SECRET GIFTS

A
HOLIDAY
NOVELLA

SATIN RUSSELL

Secret Gifts

NOTE FROM THE AUTHOR

I've had so many people reach out to me wanting to read more about Jackie and Tom, two side characters who got together in Secret Hunger.

Thank you for all the feedback. I hope you enjoy their story.

Wishing you all have a warm and wonderful holiday season.

Happy New Year!

ACKNOWLEDGMENTS

As always, thank you to my husband for dealing with my crazy and supporting me throughout.

I want to give a *big* shout-out to Lynne Favreau who did an alpha read of this novella, despite the absurdly fast turn-around.

Warm, heartfelt thanks to Chris and Holly Hammond for helping me pull a newsletter version of this novella together last year. I'm happy we've had a chance to meet and only wish we could be neighbors for longer.

CHAPTER ONE

"WHAT ABOUT THIS one? Ooh, or this one! Yeah, this one!"

Jackie laughed as her six-year-old daughter, Abby, jumped up and down, pointing at another tree. If she had her way, they'd probably buy the whole lot of them.

Crisp afternoon air nipped at the tip of Jackie's nose while her daughter inspected the tree in front of her. The blue sky was clear and bright, and despite the chill, it was a perfect winter afternoon. She'd been surprised and happy that morning when Tom suggested they get a tree after closing the café.

"I don't know, honey. The trees look too tall in this section. Let's head over to the next row," she suggested.

"Okay!" Abby ran ahead to the end of their row and disappeared around the corner. Beside her, Tom tensed and took a step forward, but Jackie held tight to his hand. "She's fine. The lot is enclosed, and it's safe. It's good for her to feel a little independent."

His shoulders lowered, and he shot her a sheepish look. "Sorry. I don't like not being able to see her."

"I love that you're protective of her—of both of us," she reassured him. Last year, their close friend and previous employer, Olivia Harper, had been stalked and kidnapped. Then, a few months later, her sister, Liz, was framed for drug trafficking and ended up having to run from the cops while trying to prove her innocence.

The past year's troubles had left him feeling anxious and on edge. His behavior reminded her of when they first met and he'd still been suffering from PTSD. She didn't blame him for his increased vigilance, but some moderation was in order.

They walked to the end of the aisle and into the next row. A gentleman with a hat low over his brow was bent down, talking to Abby, but when he spotted them, he walked away. Concern jumped in Jackie's chest, but she fought to keep it out of her voice. "Abby!"

"Oh, hi, Mommy! Look at this tree!"

She walked up to daughter. "Who were you talking to?"

Abby shrugged. "I dunno, some old guy. He asked if I was excited for Santa to come. I told him I was going to ask for a bicycle this year."

"You did?" Jackie raised her head and looked down the row of trees. Whoever had been talking to Abby was no longer in view, but she couldn't shake the feeling that he'd looked familiar. "That's nice, honey. Why don't you stick a little closer to us? Remember, we're a team."

"And teamwork makes the dream work!"

"Exactly." She raised her hand for a high five. "Now, which one did you find?"

"This one." She pointed to the tree next to her.

Tom gave Jackie's hand a squeeze before crouching to the same level as Abby. "Let's see." His black hair was a perfect contrast to her daughter's pale blonde. "Does it pass the smell test?"

The two of them angled forward and gave an exaggerated sniff. "Mmm, smells good to me," Abby confirmed.

"Let's see what your mom says."

Jackie copied their motions, playing up the act of smelling for her daughter. "Smells clean and fresh, like winter and Christmas." She pulled a glove off her hand. "How do the needles feel?" She rubbed the green spikes to release more of the sharp scent that she loved. "Not too soft, not too prickly."

"Let me lift it up and spin it around. Let's make sure there aren't any big gaps."

Though Jackie judged it to be a fairly small tree, she couldn't tamp down the thrill that ran through her as Tom grabbed the trunk and held the tree upright so they could inspect it. The man simply called to something primal in her.

"Jackie?" Tom shook her out of her musings. "How does it look?"

Abby's face shined. She clapped her hands, the sound muffled by her mittens. "This is the one! This is the one!"

"I agree. We found our tree! Good choice, Abby." She swooped her daughter up and gave her a big kiss, then shared another with Tom. Even that chaste meeting of the lips left her tingling. A sparkle in his dark eyes promised more later.

After Tom greeted the young tree-lot attendant, he told Jackie, "I'll pay for it and get it loaded onto the truck. You two go warm up in the tent with the hot chocolate and wreaths."

That was another thing which was different this year. Before she started dating Tom, Christmas-tree shopping had been a difficult and frustrating chore. A reminder that she was a single mom trying to do everything by herself.

She still remembered that first Christmas with Abby. The man at the lot had helped her get the tree secured to the roof of her car, but she hadn't considered the logistics of getting it into her modest two-bedroom rental house. It had taken her the better part of an hour to get it off the car and into the living room. The last straw was when she realized she'd forgotten to buy a tree stand and had to prop the damn thing up in a corner.

By the end of the process, she and her one-year-old were on the living room floor crying. The next year, she bought a tiny fake tree and set it on a table. Of course, then she'd felt guilty for not giving her young daughter an authentic Christmas experience.

Sometimes, there was no winning with mommy guilt.

Jackie shook her head and pushed the negative memories aside.

Fiona Harper, the youngest of the Harper Sisters, was at the counter and grinning at Abby while she topped the cup of hot chocolate with whipped cream, dusted it with chocolate, and handed it over to her. Abby's eyes were round as she carefully accepted the treat. Oh boy, somebody was going to be up late tonight.

"Fiona," she admonished, "you're going to spoil her."

"Good! That means I'm doing my job." Fiona grinned.

"Abby, what do you say?" Jackie gently reminded her daughter.

"Thank you, Auntie Fi!"

"You're welcome, sweetie. Did you find a good Christmas tree?"

"The best! It even passed the smell test."

Fiona's response was filled with delight. "Well, of course, it has to pass the smell test."

Technically, Fiona wasn't Abby's aunt, but Olivia was her oldest sister and had been Jackie's best friend since grade school. Until recently, they'd all worked at the same café that she and Tom now owned. Olivia had gone on to open a successful upscale restaurant.

Abby took a big lick of the whipped cream, which left her nose and chin white and sticky. Jackie winced. Good thing it was bath night. "Fiona, I didn't realize you were working here tonight," she said while helping her daughter take another sip.

"Be careful, it's hot. Let me get a straw for you, Abby." Fiona stuck a straw into the cup before turning to Jackie. "I got a call last minute when one of the tree-lot helpers came down with the flu. I told Herb I'd help out. He has enough on his plate managing the grocery store. Besides, it never hurts to pick up a few hours of work. Those student loans won't pay themselves, y'know."

Jackie understood what it was like to make ends meet. The Three Sisters Café had burned down a little over a year ago. When she and Tom rebuilt it and named it Abby's Café, she promised that Fiona would have a job there as long as she wanted it.

All three of the Harper Sisters—Olivia, Eliza, and Fiona—were a big part of her and Abby's life. Jackie considered them her chosen family. They were certainly closer to her than her own fundamentalist Christian parents who had abandoned her when they found out she was pregnant out of wedlock. No, the Harper sisters stuck by you through thick and thin. It was a quality Jackie never took for granted.

Not that she regretted getting pregnant. Even after her boyfriend skipped town, she considered Abby the single best thing in her life. If Abby was the only thing that asshole did right in his life, she'd take it. Her daughter was worth every second of the worry and sleepless nights.

"Hey, Fiona. How are you?" Tom said before wrapping an arm around Jackie's shoulder. His warm voice reminded her that life was better now.

"Tom, long time no see," Fiona joked. Because she worked the lunch shifts at the café five days a week, they saw each other all the time. "Would you like some hot chocolate?"

"No, thanks." To Jackie, he said, "The tree is all set. Are you ready to take off?"

She checked Abby's cup of hot chocolate and noticed it was nearly finished. Chocolate ringed her mouth, but Jackie was relieved to see none of it had managed to spill down the front of her coat. "Hey, Abby, take one last big sip and then it's time to go. We still need to get the tree set up so we can decorate it tonight."

"Okay!" Seconds later, a loud slurping sound came from the bottom of the cup, making all three adults laugh.

After saying their goodbyes, the three of them piled into the car with a brand-new Christmas tree lashed to the roof and Fiona cheerfully waving. Turning onto the street, Jackie caught a glimpse of the man from earlier standing on the edge of the lot, his hands tucked deep into his pockets.

*

Tom lay flat on his stomach, stretched out on the living room floor, and swallowed a curse as another branch poked into his shoulder.

He tightened the screw on the tree stand a few more turns. "How about now?"

"That looks better, but it's listing slightly to the right."

He focused on the next screw and twisted it. "Now?"

"Perfect! That looks straight. Let me go get some water."

He enjoyed the satisfaction in Jackie's voice. It always surprised him how easy it was to please her. If she only knew what he'd do to keep her happy.

He heard her footsteps as she re-entered the room. "Here. Be careful, it's full." He reached up for the watering can and poured the contents into the basin before crawling out from under the tree and rising to stand next to Jackie.

Jackie's hands brushed over his shoulders and back as she chuckled. "You have pine needles all over you."

He wrapped his arms around her waist, pulling her close. Her lips were soft and pliable as they met his. When he raised his head, he was gratified to see she was slightly dazed. "Are you sure you're not using it as an excuse to get your hands on me?"

"Maybe…" She smiled up at him.

"I'm hungry!" Jackie stepped out of Tom's arms as Abby came into the room.

Tom picked her up and tickled her ribs. "You are? You're hungry?"

Abby squealed and wiggled, but Tom tickled her another moment before letting go. "Lucky for you, dinner should be ready. Why don't you get your plate and silverware and put it on the table? I'll take the lasagna out of the oven."

"Yum, lasagna." She whirled into the kitchen and opened the shorter cupboard that held her plastic plate and matching utensils.

"Don't forget to put napkins on the table," Jackie reminded her. "I'll get the salad."

"Not so fast." Tom took her hand and hauled her back. "I wasn't finished with my appetizer yet." He tilted her head up, enjoying the way her breath hitched in her throat. Slowly, he bent his head but let his mouth hover, feeding the anticipation between them.

Her breasts pressed against his chest, and he could feel her rise onto her toes. He savored the moment a little longer. When neither of them could stand it, he molded his lips to hers, sweeping his tongue into her mouth. He explored the sweet recesses, tasting traces of hot chocolate, whipped cream, and something that was all Jackie.

He was pleased to hear the low moan that escaped her before easing her back. She leaned heavily against him and whispered, "No fair."

"Don't worry. I'll serve you the full course later."

"You'd better." Her eyes had deepened to the same shade of blue the sky turns when the sun sinks just below the horizon.

He loved everything about this woman and could only hope she felt the same way. Either way, he'd find out soon enough.

CHAPTER TWO

SOFT SUNLIGHT FILTERED through the opening between the bedroom curtains, creating a familiar pattern on the ceiling. At some point in the night, she'd managed to toss half the covers off, leaving one leg exposed from the calf down.

She stretched languorously, listening to Tom's deep and even breathing. Monday mornings may be greeted begrudgingly by the rest of the world, but for her, they represented a well-earned day off.

By the time they had been ready for bed last night, dinner and the dishes were finished, the Christmas lights had been strung, the ornaments hung, and the usual routine of Abby's bath, book, and bedtime observed, and neither Tom nor Jackie had energy left for 'the full course'. They'd both fallen into bed exhausted and promptly passed out.

Tom groaned and moved toward her, his heavy arm snaking around her waist and pulling her close. She snuggled deeper into his embrace and felt his desire against her backside.

Somebody was up this morning.

Clever fingers began to explore, ducking under her tank top and caressing her belly. She ground her ass tighter against his body, rubbing into his hard-on, but he refused to be rushed. He cupped her breast, weighing it in his hand, before sliding his thumb along the sensitive bottom curve. With the barest of touches, his fingertips skimmed the ring of her areola until her nipple puckered into a hard, needy nub.

Her breath caught when he gave it a pinch. The welcome sting sparked her nerve endings and had her back arching. Desire pooled between her legs. The low growl in his throat was edged with sinful intent. He nipped her earlobe then trailed his lips along her nape, sending goosebumps fluttering through her system and down her arms.

His mouth continued its path downward, over her shoulder. All the while, his fingers continued to knead and cup her breasts. From behind, he tucked his knee between hers and spread her legs open so that she was pressed against his chest and vulnerable to his ministrations. All her attention was focused on his hand as it dipped into the waistband of her panties. He spread her outer lips and ran fingers through her slick passion before fluttering over the knot of nerves that begged for his attention. Her whole body tensed like a bow as he drew tiny circles over her flesh.

Pressure built, winding tighter and tighter. She rocked and strained into his touch, but he held on, securing her against his body. Her pulse pounded as every molecule was focused solely on where he touched her. She struggled to hang on even as she reveled in the build-up and anticipation of her desire.

One finger delved into her entrance, testing her readiness, and she panted. "Please, please…" she pleaded, not afraid to show him how much she needed him.

He added a second finger, which was more satisfying but still not enough. She groaned as his thumb continued to work her clitoris, and his fingers found the secret spot deep inside, and then everything exploded until she was gasping and quivering in his arms. He laid his hand flat against her mound and let her slowly drift down from her climax.

As she came to her senses, she could feel his erection hard against her back, and what had been satisfaction morphed into greater need. She longed to be filled. His fingers were enough to tease but not enough to quench the heat and pressure that had built up inside of her. His other hand caught her hair, angling her head for his kiss before he rose above her body.

He quickly discarded her tank top before snagging her panties and dragging them down her legs. His large hands gripped her hips and reeled her closer, spreading her thighs and exposing everything to his view. The corners of his mouth curved when he gently thumbed her sensitive bud and watched her jump. She loved how he could calibrate every part of her to his whim.

His other hand stroked his long length before he bent over her and captured her nipple between his lips. She gasped.

As he guided his way into her, her legs eagerly wrapped around his waist, but his tip teased her entrance. Brushing her sweat-dampened hair from her forehead, Tom watched her face as he entered her, inch by torturous inch. Finally, he was seated deep within her body with one long push. They both shuddered. Every corner of her felt consumed by the man above her.

And then he began to move, rebuilding and stoking the pressure and heat that had been spent moments earlier. Each thrust was measured and disciplined—utterly maddening. His passion remained tightly contained while Jackie writhed beneath him.

Her inner muscles clenched around him as he drew his length slowly out. Every stroke pushing and pulling, giving and receiving. She could feel his arms trembling with the strain of control. A long, low moan came from somewhere deep in her soul, and the sound frayed what little restraint Tom had left.

His hips shot forward, over and over, driving them both up to the crest of their pleasure before catapulting them over the edge. Jackie bit his shoulder, stifling the screams that begged to be released, some part of her still aware of her daughter a few doors down. The self-control intensified the sensations that racked her body until even the ends of her hair felt electrified.

It was tempting to drift back to sleep as they both lay sweaty and satisfied in each other's arms, but soon necessity had her standing and heading to the bathroom. Once finished, she gave Tom a lingering kiss before pulling on a tank top and yoga pants. A fuzzy robe and her beloved bunny slippers completed her lazy-morning outfit.

She was sad to notice her slippers were a bit worse for wear and wondered how much longer they'd last. They were the same ones she wore that day a year ago when Tom had knocked on her door with soup and cold medicine. Olivia loved to tease her and say that was the day he 'hopped into her heart'.

Jackie poked her head into Abby's bedroom and stifled a chuckle when she noticed her arms flung to either side. All the covers were bunched up at the bottom of the mattress. No question whom she got her sleeping habits from. Like mother, like daughter.

After carefully straightening Abby's blankets, she shuffled into the kitchen and put a pot of coffee on. The Christmas tree stood in the front corner of the living room, framed by windows on either wall. It was full of crafted ornaments, including her favorite one with Abby's smudged handprint from her first Christmas. She bent down and plugged the tree in, admiring the effect.

White lights were strung up the center and down the outside, which Tom insisted was the only correct way of doing them. Red and silver balls hung at regular intervals, and garlands of red and silver beads completed the homey picture. It wasn't a big tree, but what it lacked in stature it made up for in heart.

Jackie loved it.

The beeping of the coffeemaker promised caffeine and lucidity. She brought down the oversized red mugs she liked to use during this time of year because they had a snowflake pattern. As she began to pour, two strong arms snaked around her waist.

"You're lucky I've got a steady hand," she said, leaning against the hard chest behind her.

Tom moved her closer and nipped her earlobe. "Mmm, you're right, I am."

It took a little more concentration not to spill the strong brew when he kissed down the length of her neck, but she didn't mind. Sometimes, it was difficult to believe she got to wake up with this man every morning.

If anyone would have suggested she'd be here a year and a half ago, she would have told them they were crazy. She and Tom had worked together for years, but she had no idea he'd harbored romantic feelings for her the whole time.

She'd always assumed that such a quiet and intense person wouldn't possibly be attracted to someone like her. Her life was loud and hectic and crazy and completely disorganized. Half the time, she didn't know what she was doing or what she was feeling. How could a man who kept his emotions so contained want a life like that?

Jackie turned and ran her hands up Tom's arms, stopping to revel in the strength of his biceps before looping them behind his neck. His eyes were the color of her favorite dark roast and currently warm with desire. They shot a jolt through her system that was stronger and hotter than any cup of coffee. His hands traced the sides of her waist, sending shivers down her spine, and she raised her mouth for another kiss.

Maybe they should have stayed in bed.

Pounding at the front door made them jump. Tom's muscles tightened beneath her hands as he raised his head. He rushed toward the door as another spate of knocking blasted the morning's peace.

After checking the peephole, Tom opened the door, his large frame blocking the person from Jackie's view.

"Can I help you?" She suppressed amusement at the way Tom's voice had deepened with irritation. If this was a missionary or political canvasser, they certainly had their work cut out for them.

"I want to speak to Jackie."

What? Who would want to see her so badly that they'd pound on the door this early, especially on a Monday morning? Any of her friends would know better. She peeked past Tom's shoulder, but he didn't move. If anything, his stance grew broader.

"Who are you?" Tom asked.

"Let me talk to her. I know she's here." Something about the other man's voice scratched at her memory, but she couldn't quite place it. Then it hit her.

"Randy?"

Tom glanced back over his shoulder at her. "You know him?"

She bit her bottom lip, trepidation sitting in the pit of her stomach. At one time, she thought she knew him. She'd been mistaken. Placing a hand on Tom's shoulder, she stepped forward. "What are you doing here, Randy?"

He'd been a fairly good-looking guy when they were younger. Your typical clean-cut, upper middle-class, suburban white boy whose family went to the same conservative church her family attended.

It was hard to believe it had been a little over six years ago since she'd last seen him. Those days felt like they belonged to a different person from a different life. Now, his sandy-brown hair was shot through with gray and thinning on top. The fine web of wrinkles sprouting from the corners of his eyes made him look like he was constantly squinting.

He plastered on his best smile, but all she could see was the way his teeth were faded to a dingy yellow. She remembered the way his crooked smirk had been endearing. How naïve she'd been.

"Hiya, Jackie." His gaze roved down her front, making her feel exposed, despite her fleece robe and bunny slippers. "You're looking good."

She could practically hear Tom's teeth grinding behind her. There was no way she was going to be able to have a conversation with the two of them glaring at each other. Turning to him, she placed a hand on Tom's chest. "Give me a minute to talk to him."

His formidable scowl was redirected toward her. "What?"

"Please. It's better if I get to the bottom of this as soon as possible, which might be easier if I can talk to him alone."

He searched her face before relenting. "Are you sure?" With her assurance, he stepped back. "I'll be inside if you need anything."

"Thank you." She gave him a light kiss before pulling the door closed behind her. Crossing her arms, she wrapped her robe securely around her and focused on Randy.

"He sure has you on a short leash, don't he?"

Whatever benefit of the doubt Jackie was willing to give the father of her child died at his comment. She pursed her lips. "You have two minutes to tell me what the hell you are doing here. Then you better get off my property before I call the cops."

He raised his hands. "Okay, okay, I'm sorry! I didn't realize it was such a touchy subject for you."

What did she ever see in this guy? "Time's ticking."

The wide-eyed, earnest look on his face would have fooled her at one time. Now, it had the opposite effect and put her on guard. Still, she owed it to her daughter to hear what he had to say. "I've been doing a lot of thinking."

With that, he let out a big sigh and ran a hand through his hair. "I admit I did wrong by you when I left six years ago. Believe me when I tell you that I've regretted my actions ever since. Neither you nor our daughter deserved to be treated that way."

Where was this coming from? And why now? "Tell me something I don't know."

He winced as if she'd hit him. He slouched a little lower. "I deserve that. After I left, I went to a bad place. I started drinking heavily and made a bigger mess of my life. Got into a spot of trouble here and there. I'm ashamed to admit, I even spent some time in jail. But a couple of months ago, I was released early for good behavior. Part of my parole agreement was that I had to keep attending AA meetings."

While Jackie couldn't say she was surprised by the trajectory his life had taken, she was happy to hear he was turning himself around. "Good for you."

He nodded, making sure to keep his gaze locked on hers. "Thank you."

She shifted on her feet, uncomfortable with the look he was giving her. "Not to be rude, but what does that have to do with me?"

Randy scuffed the bottom of his shoes on the front step. "Part of the program I'm in talks about making reparations for the damage and hurt you've caused the people around you. Leaving you, especially when you needed me most, has been the single biggest mistake of my life, and I wanted to tell you that I'm sorry. I'd like to make it up to you if I can. I'm also hoping you'll let me make it up to my daughter."

The ground fell out from under her, and her gut clenched. She'd toiled for six years—*six years*—without him. No way was this bastard getting near her daughter. He didn't deserve her sweetness or to bask in her light. What made him think he had the right to come here and reap the rewards of all her hard work? The lump in her throat refused to let any words pass.

Clearly oblivious to her inner turmoil, he forged on. His brow wrinkled in remorse. "Hell, I'm not even sure what her name is. I should know what my own daughter's name is. Did you name her Abby like you said you would?"

He didn't even know her name. Fury and sorrow filled her as she thought about her beautiful little girl. The way she wrinkled her nose when she was concentrating, the way her hair smelled after a bath, or how she'd beg for another bedtime story.

She remembered all the nights she'd stayed up rocking her, begging her to fall asleep. Or the way she squealed when Jackie would blow raspberries on her belly. All the good times and the struggles to get her to where she was now. All the milestones Jackie was still looking forward to.

Randy didn't deserve those, but didn't her daughter deserve to have a father in her life to share them with?

Jackie took a deep breath and counted to three before she tamped down her temper and tried to consider what was best for Abby. The last thing she wanted was for Abby to grow up and resent her for keeping her from having a relationship with him.

However, that didn't mean she was prepared to hand her daughter over to him, either. He needed to offer some proof that he was responsible and reliable. She needed to confirm he was going to take this role seriously.

"Yes, her name is Abby." She rubbed the spot between her brows that always gathered tension when she was stressed. "Let me consider it, Randy."

"But—"

She raised a hand. "No. This is all very sudden for me. You may have been planning this request for a while, but from where I'm standing, it's coming out of the blue. I don't want to get Abby's hopes up only for you to disappear and disappoint her. Believe it or not, she's done perfectly fine without you in her life. I won't have you inflicting irreparable damage to her." At his crestfallen face, she continued. "I'm not saying no. I'm saying let me think about the parameters for your introduction and visitation. That's only fair."

"Fine, Jackie. Whatever you feel is best." His resigned tone made it obvious that it wasn't the answer he was looking for, but Jackie wasn't going to apologize for not catering to his request right away. With a visible effort to change the subject, he continued. "So, uh, I hear things have been going pretty well for you. I saw your name in the paper a couple of months ago. Something about you opening a new café?"

A leery sense of unease caused her to re-cross her arms. Was that why he was here? Surely not. Like he'd said, that was months ago! Besides, nobody ever got rich running a small-town café. "We're doing all right."

He rubbed a hand behind his neck and gave her what he must have considered an ingratiating smile. She stared at him and fought to remember why she'd ever been attracted. His round shoulders and weak chin merely hinted at the questionable character at his foundation.

An image of Tom's intense focus as he moved above her that morning flashed through her mind, and she shivered. If she'd stayed with Randy, the trajectory of her life would have been incredibly different. They'd grown up in a community where every expectation—every goal—had been laid out and defined for her.

The fact she had gotten pregnant before getting married had devastated her parents. And when she told them that she wasn't going to marry Randy, the entire church had ostracized her. Unable to take the heat, Randy had skipped town, leaving her to fend for herself.

And though she'd never admit it, some part of her still had a hard time keeping her head up when she ran into members of her former congregation. Thankfully, it didn't happen very often. Even in a small town, she'd become an expert at avoiding certain people.

"How long are you going to make me wait before I can see my daughter?"

"You're assuming I'll say yes." Ignoring his combative tone, she took her phone out of the pocket of her robe. "Give me your number and I'll call you in a couple of days to let you know what I decide."

His lips thinned with disappointment, and Jackie had to fight the urge to apologize. Why did she still feel driven to please the people around her? She stood taller. Not this time. Not when it came to her daughter.

After gathering his contact information, including the apartment number in the boarding house he was staying at, she went back into the house, quietly shutting the door behind her. She leaned back against it and closed her eyes, trying to take in the ramifications of what had happened.

Abby's voice floated in from the kitchen along with Tom's

deeper, melodic tones. "Nice smiley face, Abby. What should we make for your mom?"

"I know. How about a kitty!"

"Good idea. Let's do it."

When she stepped into the room, she found them bent over a carefully poured pancake with a row of chocolate chips lined up on the counter. Setting aside the earlier events, she made sure to keep her voice bright and cheerful. "Hey, guys, what's going on in here?"

"Mommy, Mommy! We're making chocolate chip pancakes!"

"You are!" She examined the pile of pancakes already on the plate. "Wow, looks like you've been busy."

Tom gave her a look that was full of questions and concern. She shook her head, indicating they'd talk about the conversation later.

She wrapped her arms around Abby. "You know what I haven't gotten from you yet? A good-morning hug!" She squeezed her close and relished the feel of Abby's arms around her neck.

Jackie would have held her for longer, but a moment later, her little body wiggled impatiently. "Mommy, we have to put the chocolate chips in."

She sighed. "Go on, then. I'll set the table."

Her daughter nodded. "Good idea."

Gathered around the table with the two people she loved most, Jackie struggled to put the conversation with Randy out of her mind. There would be plenty of time to get Tom's input. If she decided to grant his request, they'd need to plan for Abby's introduction to Randy. She watched as Abby poured a small ocean of syrup onto her plate.

"You want some pancake with your syrup?" Tom teased.

Abby put the bottle down, although Jackie noticed she kept it close.

"Guess what we have planned for today?" Jackie said.

"What?" her daughter mumbled.

She chose not to remind her daughter not to talk with her

mouth full. Sometimes, you had to pick your battles. "Auntie Livvy invited us over to make Christmas cookies."

"*She did?*" Abby bounced in her chair. Olivia always went all-out when making cookies, and Jackie knew today would be no exception.

"Yes, she did. We should put a couple of baskets together, one for your teacher and one for the school bake sale."

"Okay, but can we still keep a few?"

She looked so concerned that Jackie stifled a laugh. "Of course. Auntie Livvy has plenty for everyone."

Jackie finished her cup of coffee and debated whether to take another pancake. Before she could talk herself out of it, Tom reached over and dropped one on her plate. This one was a butterfly.

"You two eat up. I'll do the dishes while you get ready."

"Are you going to come over with us?" Jackie asked. She always wanted Tom around, but Randy being in town made her want it even more.

"I promised Mason I'd help him with an errand, but it should only take a couple of hours. I'll give you a ride over and be there in time to bring you home."

"That works." She watched Abby trace patterns in the syrup with her fork. "Remember, sweetie, the sooner we finish breakfast, the sooner we can head over."

Jackie wasn't sure whether to laugh or admonish her when Abby stuffed her mouth with the rest of her pancake.

CHAPTER THREE

TOM SWALLOWED AND fought the urge to spin around and walk back out. Glass cases glowed and sparkled in the gallery lighting as he and Mason stepped into the jewelry store, lingering on the threshold.

"Wow, look at all of this. Where should we begin?" Mason paused. "This is a big step, man. You sure you're ready?"

"About Jackie? Yes. About picking out one of these rings?" Tom looked around.

"Hello, gentlemen. My name is Gemma." A well-manicured woman in her forties approached them. Her warm and professional appearance immediately put Tom at ease. "Can I help you with something specific?"

"I hope so." Tom cleared his throat. "I'm looking for an engagement ring for my girlfriend."

"How exciting! Congratulations."

"Thanks. Well, I haven't asked her yet…" Tom's mind filled with worst-case scenarios.

"…but she's definitely going to say yes," Mason added. The surety in his friend's voice helped quell Tom's doubts.

"I'm sure she's a very lucky woman," the salesperson replied. "Did you have some styles in mind, or would you like to look around and see what inspires you?"

Tom looked to Mason, who raised his hands. "Don't look at me. I don't know the first thing about rings."

He glanced at the cases. "I'd like to see what you have available."

"You're more than welcome to look. How experienced are you with buying jewelry?"

"Not much, to be honest," Tom admitted.

"Don't worry, you're not alone," Gemma reassured him. "The key concepts you want to keep in mind are the four Cs."

"Four Cs?"

"Yes." She raised her hand and ticked them off. "Cut, color, clarity, and carat." Gemma proceeded to expound on each of the points.

"It should be called the five Cs. Don't wanna forget about 'cost'," Mason added. Tom was happy to see he wasn't the only one paying attention.

"That's also an important consideration," Gemma agreed.

"Right. Five Cs." He looked at Mason. "We can handle that."

"Great! How about I give you a few minutes to check the rings out, and I'll come back and see what questions you have. Most of our engagement rings are in this center section."

They walked over to the cases she indicated and peered at the selection. After a moment of deliberation, Tom rubbed his forehead. "I want it to be perfect, y'know?"

"Hey, man, I get it. Trust me, you're not the only one who's been contemplating rings."

"Really?" Tom digested the news and grinned. "Luckily for you, I'll be an expert by the time you ask Olivia."

Mason slapped him on the shoulder. "That's what I'm counting on." He gestured to the display in front of him. "Some of these are way over-the-top. I don't see either one of them being interested in something this gaudy."

"Probably a good thing since they cost more than my truck."

Mason chuckled. "True, but who would want to wear them, anyway?"

"Jackie tends to lean more toward a classic look but nothing boring." He lifted a shoulder. "I feel like I'll recognize it when I see it."

"That sounds about right."

Gemma rejoined them. "Have you found any you'd like to take a closer look at?" she asked.

"There's so many of them." Tom pointed to the case they stood by. "She wouldn't go for any of those, though."

"Not modern, then. That's good." She gave him an encouraging smile. "Sometimes, it's easier to identify what someone wouldn't like than what they would like. Why don't you tell me a little about her? I can help direct you to a style that would suit her personality. First off, what's her name?"

By the time Tom finished describing Jackie and her tastes, they had whittled the choices down to three. Two were simple solitaires, but the last one had more flourish and seemed innately feminine. As another young couple walked into the store, Gemma excused herself to greet them, leaving Tom and Mason to decide which ring setting to go with.

"What do you think of this last one, Mason?"

"I think she's gonna love it," he said.

The ring had a center diamond surrounded by a layer of smaller diamonds. It was made of rose gold and had a delicate halo setting. The overall effect looked like a flower. It was classic and timeless but still unique. Just like Jackie.

Tome inspected it further. "I agree. She didn't have a lot of frills growing up. Her parents were pretty strict about certain things, vanity being one of them."

"Olivia has told me about some of it. Sounds like a sad way to be raised."

"It's probably why she tends to indulge Abby." He hesitated. "Hey, I've gotta ask you a favor." Once he was sure he had Mason's full attention, he continued. "We had an unwelcome visitor stop by the house this morning."

"You did? Who?"

Tom looked down at the ring in front of him but didn't see it. He remembered the stress lines framing Jackie's tense mouth like parentheses when she'd joined him and Abby in the kitchen. "Abby's biological father."

Mason let out a low whistle. "No shit?"

"He says he wants to get back into Abby's life. He's asking for visitation rights."

"Damn. That takes some balls." Rubbing his chin, he added under his breath, "Bastard."

Tom liked that about Mason. He had your back, no questions asked. In Tom's experience, it was a rare quality, and he felt lucky to have Mason as a friend. "My thoughts exactly."

Tom ran a hand through his hair. "I was planning on asking Jackie if I could adopt Abby, assuming she says yes to my proposal. I'm not sure how that's going to work out with Randy back in the picture." A pang in his heart had him rubbing his chest. He loved that little girl as if she were his own and had been looking forward to sharing his last name with her.

The look Mason shot him said he knew what Tom was going to ask. "Let me do a background check on him when I go into work. I'd feel better confirming his story checks out, at least."

"Thanks, man. I appreciate it."

Mason clapped a hand on his shoulder. "Of course. Olivia and I love those two. They're family. All of you are. I've never met this asshole, but we're going to make sure he doesn't fuck anything up."

Relief loosened the muscles in Tom's neck and back.

Gemma rejoined them. "Sorry about that. Have you made a decision?"

Tom handed her the setting he'd chosen. "This is the one." He pulled out a ring he'd swiped from Jackie's jewelry box. "I wasn't sure what ring size she is, but this fits her."

"I'm glad to see you're prepared." She took the ring from him. "Now that we have the setting picked out, let's go look at some diamonds!"

Mason and Tom's eyes grew round. This visit was going to take longer than expected.

*

"Can you hand me the red sprinkles, please?" Abby asked sweetly.

"Here you go." Olivia gave her the little canister then watched as she upended half the contents over the cookie on her plate. "That looks great, Abby!"

"Thanks." She bent down and started gently brushing the fine sugar crystals with her index finger.

Jackie loved seeing her daughter fully immersed in a project, and this time was no exception. "Is that the gingerbread man's shirt?"

She nodded. "Uh-huh."

Jackie noticed that Abby's apron was covered in flour and smears of frosting. It was a good thing she'd remembered to bring one.

"This is so much fun, Olivia. Thank you for putting it together. I'm not sure how I would have gotten everything finished before the bake sale. That reminds me, do you still plan on coming to the school this Friday? The bake sale is at four, and the recital starts at five."

"Are you kidding me? Mason and I wouldn't miss it." She looked at Abby. "Are you excited?"

"Yup! I even get to shake real sleigh bells when we sing 'Jingle Bells'!"

"Wow, that's going to sound amazing," Olivia said.

Jackie shot her friend a wry grimace. "She's been very good at practicing."

"I'm sure." Olivia's expression held a hint of sympathy and humor. "I love baking Christmas cookies with you guys!"

Jackie loved that about Olivia. She made people feel good about themselves. It reminded her of the time she'd asked about taking over Olivia's café. By the time Jackie was finished making her proposal, she had felt like she was the one doing Olivia a favor—not the other way around.

Although, if she were being fair, they had been helping each other out of bad situations ever since grade school. Remembering those memories and seeing how far they'd both come made Jackie feel nostalgic.

Impulsively, she flung her arms around Olivia and gave her a tight squeeze.

The frosting Olivia was carefully applying to the gingerbread man created a jagged line across his neck. "Hey!" She laughed. "What was that for?"

"I don't know. Maybe because you're wonderful."

"Aw, shucks." Olivia gave her a quick hug before finishing the frosting. Somehow, she managed to make the zigzag look intentional.

"Your cookies look amazing." Jackie glanced down at her own gingerbread man. His face was off-kilter and gave the unfortunate impression that he'd been hitting the eggnog a little too hard.

Olivia brushed the compliment off. "Lots and lots of practice." She searched Jackie's face, concern hiding in the corners of her mouth. "No, seriously. What's up?"

Tears threatened, but Jackie blinked them back. The lump in her throat was harder to overcome. "I can't talk about it at the moment."

Her friend bent closer and lowered her voice. "Does it have something to do with Tom? How are you two doing?"

Jackie sniffled. "No, no, Tom and I are fine. Although, he's concerned about me. I had a visitor this morning. You'll never guess who."

Olivia chewed her bottom lip, her brows wrinkled. After a moment she said, "You're right. I have no idea."

"Look, Mommy!" Abby held her gingerbread man up for inspection.

"How festive! He looks very dashing in his red coat and pants."

"I made him into Santa Claus." Her daughter beamed.

"And what a fine-looking Santa Claus he is," Olivia confirmed. "Why don't you put him on the cookie sheet with all the other finished ones? Then you can taste-test one of these with a glass of milk. What do you say?"

"Yes!" Abby wiggled in her chair, energy practically exploding out of her. Jackie shook her head. The last thing she needed was a sugar rush.

"Go take a bathroom break and wash your hands first. Then you can have one—one—cookie," she instructed.

"Okay!" She clamored down from her chair and raced to the restroom down the hall. Jackie couldn't help but smile.

It was short-lived. Olivia said, "You have five, make that three minutes to spill. What's going on?"

As quickly as possible, Jackie told her friend about finding Randy at her front door and their talk that morning.

Olivia gasped. "*He wants what?* How dare he!"

Groaning, Jackie put her head in her hands, giving up all pretense of maintaining composure. "Exactly! But who am I to keep Abby away from her father?"

Olivia gave a disgusted snort. "Sperm donor perhaps, but I'd hardly call him a father." She walked to the refrigerator and poured Abby a cup of milk. "Besides, can he even do that? It's not like he's been paying child support. If he pushes the issue, I'm sure you could fight him in court and win."

"I'm not sure about that. Everything I've heard regarding cases like this is that they default heavily toward keeping the biological parents in the kids' lives. Besides, even if I could keep him away from her, the question is, should I?"

"I'm ready!" Abby skated back into the kitchen, her socked feet sliding easily on the hardwood floor.

"You're right on time. Which of these lovely gingerbread men would you like to decapitate today?" Olivia asked.

Abby giggled and pointed out a poor, hapless cookie.

"Excellent choice, m'dear." Olivia placed it on a plate in front of her. "Ooh, he's still warm. Enjoy!" She made eye contact with Jackie over the top of Abby's head. "We're overdue for a girls' night. Let's plan something for this week."

"That sounds perfect." Snatching a cookie from the pile, Jackie took a big bite, adding, "Did I mention I love you?"

CHAPTER FOUR

JACKIE BALANCED A tray with three plates and held another in her hand as she rounded the counter. Dodging a man as he pushed back his chair, she sidestepped to the group of women on their lunch break.

"Here you are, ladies. A BLT for you, Connie. Shaina, one turkey on rye. And club sandwiches for Heather and Lindsay. Bri and Noelle aren't with you today?"

"Noelle is still on vacation in Paris, and Bri took the day off. Did you hear she got a new puppy?" Lindsay asked.

"I did! The photos are adorable." She took a bottle of ketchup out of her apron pocket. "Ketchup for the fries... I'll be right back with a refill on your soda. Did you want some more ice tea, Heather?"

"Yes, please. I don't know how you make it, but I'm addicted to it."

"It's nothing fancy. I could give you the recipe." Jackie gave the table another glance. "Is there anything else I can get you?"

"Nope, this looks great! Thanks, Jackie," Shaina answered.

"You're welcome. Enjoy." She picked up a menu and went to greet the quiet-looking man who walked in. "Hello, would you like a table or a seat at the counter?"

"Neither. Are you Jackie Davis?"

"Yes, that's me." Her expression wilted as he handed her a thick envelope.

"You've been served."

All the air was sucked out of her lungs. By the time she could respond, he'd already left.

"Are you feeling all right, Jackie? You look a little pale," Fiona asked as she bussed a table nearby.

"Wha—Oh, yeah." She gazed around the dining room, trying to figure out what she was supposed to be doing, the envelope clutched in her hand. "Actually, no. Fiona, can you bring a refill over to table four? They'd like a soda and an ice tea. I have to take a minute."

Concern wrinkled her brow. "Of course."

"Thanks." Jackie's chin trembled while she weaved between the tables and struggled to maintain her composure. Finally, she reached her office and shut the restaurant out behind her. Instantly, her emotions took over.

That son of a bitch! She pounded a fist against the door. He must have started the proceedings before he'd shown up on her front step yesterday morning with his shit-eating grin and air of contrition.

Her hands shook as she tore open the envelope and read the papers. Each word made her stomach sink lower. The bastard wasn't merely seeking visitation rights. He was filing for joint custody.

A sob escaped. So much for taking things slow. How was she going to explain this to Abby? Their lives finally felt like they were humming along. She should have expected something would throw a wrench in it.

The knock on the door made her jump. Dashing the tears from her cheeks, she pasted on a smile and answered. Tom stood in the doorway, his face filled with concern. "What's wrong?"

Her mask faltered then disappeared as tears began to fall. "He filed for joint custody."

She didn't quite catch the words said under his breath, but the tone was vicious. Tom stepped into the small room and shut the door behind him. He searched her face. "Come here."

The knot in her chest loosened as she curled up against him. His strong arms tightened around her and he rubbed her back. She took a deep breath, trying to gain control of her emotions. "I can't figure out why he's gung-ho all of a sudden. He had no interest in being a father when I was pregnant or in the past six years."

"Shh, it'll be okay."

Her voice climbed in pitch. "How? How can this possibly be okay?" She gave up trying to calm herself down.

Tom was silent long enough that she began to wonder if he would answer. When he did, he spoke matter-of-factly. "The courts might go for visitation rights, but I doubt they'll be willing to grant him joint custody right off the bat, especially since he hasn't had any contact with her for the first six years of her life. Add the fact that he hasn't paid any child support, and I'm guessing he doesn't have a very strong case."

Logically, everything he said made sense, but Jackie couldn't shake the sinking feeling she had.

He continued. "My guess is that he's trying to intimidate you into conceding before it gets to court. We're going to need a good family lawyer."

Jackie fought the urge to scream. The last thing she could afford was another financial setback. She'd spent most of her savings getting the café up and running after the fire destroyed it. Even then, Tom had put up the lion's share of the cost.

"I have a couple of savings bonds that were given to me when Abby was born. I can probably cash those out." She stepped out of Tom's arms and slapped the hateful papers down on the desk. The chair squeaked as she sank into it. "I don't care if I have to dance on a pole, I refuse to touch her college fund. That is absolutely off-limits."

"As tempting as that image is, we can avoid that." Strong fingers began to stroke the knots out of her shoulders. "You can count on me to help."

"I can't ask you to do that." Jackie let her head fall forward into her hands and moaned when he dug into a particularly tight spot. Suddenly, she sat up straight. "Wait, who's in the kitchen right now?"

"Relax. I called Olivia the minute I saw you storm back here and knew something was wrong. She has the night off at the restaurant and said she'd finish my shift for me. Fiona has the front of the house."

She groaned as he dug into another knot. "Thank goodness. What would we do without those sisters?" A tremor raced through her system. "I know for a fact a couple of people overheard the process server when he handed me those papers. I don't think I can go back out there and function. I can imagine what the rumor mill is churning out."

"Don't worry. Olivia said she owed me one." Jackie nodded. He'd covered a lot of early morning shifts for her last winter, when Olivia and Mason were dealing with a stalker. "Come on. We might as well take advantage of the extra time off and do something productive. Let's get out of here."

It felt weird, but she gathered her things, put on her coat, and slipped out the back door, grateful to be leaving.

"Where do you want to go?" Tom asked.

"Home. I want to climb into bed and pretend none of this happened."

He grasped her hand. "We can do that."

"I wish we could, but we can't." She sighed and pressed her head back against the seat. "You were right. I have to hire a good family lawyer, which means I need to go to the bank."

"Maybe after that, we can climb into bed and pretend the world doesn't exist."

Jackie laughed. "No, then it will be time to pick up Abby from school."

He snapped his fingers. "That's right. I knew I was forgetting something." He winked. "If we can't bury our heads in the sand, let's make these hours work for us."

For some reason, even though nothing had been resolved, Jackie felt better. When they stopped at a red light, she placed a hand on his arm. "Hey."

He shifted his attention from the light. "Yeah?"

"Thank you."

She nuzzled his hand as he cupped her cheek. "I'll always have your back."

CHAPTER FIVE

THE TWO EXTRA hours were eaten up at the bank, but Tom knew that Jackie felt more in control once she had her finances in order. He repeatedly offered to help pay the lawyer fees, but she'd refused him every time.

The fact she was determined to keep their money separate felt like a dagger to the heart. Logically, he realized she was doing it out of pride and self-respect. But as far as he was concerned, they were family and he couldn't imagine life without the two of them.

If only he could get Jackie to realize it.

Tom drove his truck up to the circle in front of the elementary school and parked, making sure to leave some room behind the school buses. It wasn't the first time he'd picked Abby up.

"Looks like we're a few minutes early," Jackie said. "Hey, there's Amy."

A pretty woman with shoulder-length, light brown hair waved. Her son was in the same class as Abby, and after-school pick-ups gave them a chance to talk while they waited. Jackie put on what Tom referred to as her 'good mom face' and opened the door. "I'm going to say hello and review the details of the bake sale with her. I know, as the PTA president, she regrets not being able to head it up this year, but honestly—look at her! She'll be lucky if that baby doesn't pop out at the recital!"

"Hell, let's hope not." Tom shuddered. "I'll stay here."

She bent over the console and gave him a kiss, letting her lips linger on his for a second more than he'd expected. "I love you."

He brushed a strand of hair off her cheek. It didn't matter how often she said it, his heart squeezed each time he heard her say those words. "I love you, too."

She stepped out of the car and walked over to the other moms who were gathered. He liked how she made a point to greet everyone by name and ask how they were doing.

Her kindness was one of the qualities that first attracted him. She would direct comments or questions his way, or ask for his opinion. He wasn't much of a talker and was used to blending in and going unnoticed by people.

But never by her.

He gripped the steering wheel. It pissed him off the way life worked against good people. Why did the assholes get ahead while the nice people, the ones who tried to make life better, seemed to get all the hard knocks?

With that idea in mind, he called Mason. After two rings, he picked up.

"Hey, man. I was going to call you later today."

"Have you found anything about Randy?"

"Nothing he didn't already mention to Jackie. He did do a stint in the county jail for one count of drunk and disorderly and two counts of vandalism, but they were fairly minor charges and he got off with community service. He also served some time for assault. Looks like it was alcohol-related."

"Would any of that prevent him from getting joint custody of Abby?"

Mason sucked in a breath. "Are you kidding me?"

"Afraid not."

"The assault charge could pose a serious problem for him. On the other hand, a half-decent lawyer would probably gain some leeway if he can prove he's getting help. You said he told Jackie he's in Alcoholics Anonymous and working the steps, right?"

"Yeah."

"Damn, man. That's hard to call. I'm going to say he has an uphill battle, but it's not impossible."

Tom groaned. "That's what I was afraid of."

"Look, everything I've told you is easy information to find. I put a few other feelers out, but those will take a bit longer to get back to me. I'll tell you if I discover anything useful."

"I appreciate it."

"Do me a favor. Keep your head about you, Tom. Don't do anything that will make the situation worse."

He gritted his teeth. "I have no idea what you're talking about."

"That's what I thought."

Commotion at the school door caused him to look up. "Son of a bitch, hang on a sec."

"What's going—" but Tom was already halfway out of the cab, phone held down by his side.

Randy had dragged Jackie away from the group, and the two of them were talking under their breaths, their tones terse.

"Take your hand off her." Tom's voice was low, the warning clear.

Rage built in his chest when the other man's fingers tightened on her bicep. Jackie winced but struggled to hide it. She was clearly trying to keep a low profile in front of the other mothers. As it was, her cheeks were two bright flags of embarrassment. Amy and a few of the women had their heads bent toward each other. He could practically see a cloud of questions and conjectures floating over them.

Tom stepped closer. "Let. Go."

Sneering, Randy let go and raked his gaze up and down Tom. "Geez, Jackie. I see you've lowered your standards." His lip curled. "As if this jackass could keep me away from my daughter."

Jackie gasped, outrage suffusing her face.

"I've been called worse from bigger assholes than you," Tom growled. "And until you do get permission from the courts, you have no right to be here." He lifted his phone to his ear. "Detective Mason, you still there?"

"I'm here. Would you like me to send someone over?"

"Thanks, but I think we have it under control." Tom's eyes were molten pits.

"I'm keeping my phone close by. Let me know if that changes."

"Will do." He hung up before stuffing his phone in his back pocket. His gaze stayed pinned on the other man.

Randy's neck grew ruddy with anger. He loomed toward Jackie, but Tom noticed he didn't dare touch her again. "The courts are going to hear all about this," he hissed. "I'm sure they'll be very interested in knowing how you bring strange men into the house and around our daughter."

The color drained from Jackie's face, but she straightened her shoulders. "You have no idea what you're talking about."

"I know that your loose morals are setting a piss-poor example for her. We'll be lucky if she doesn't grow up to be a little slut like you."

Before Tom could react, a loud crack rent the air as Jackie's palm met Randy's cheek. Silence reigned as every parent in attendance held their breath.

Tom had never seen Jackie in such a state. She was breathing hard, her eyes narrowed and filled with righteous anger. It would have been a glorious sight if not for the circumstances.

"Looks like I'm not the only one prone to assaulting someone." Randy's expression morphed from shock to smug victory, filling Tom with dread. "Loose morals and violent. My lawyer is going to have a field day with you."

The double front doors of the school opened, releasing the sound of children shrieking with glee. Tom stepped in front of Randy before he had a chance to move. He raised a hand. "Don't."

It didn't hurt that he stood over Randy by a good four inches, but Tom knew that wasn't why the other man stopped. The violence he'd labored and fought to push down after the war had reawoken. Every molecule of his being wanted nothing more than to snap this bastard's neck. His fingers twitched with the memory of how easily those bones could break.

The need to inflict violence rose up and nearly consumed him while echoes of gunfire and war had him gritting his teeth. He fought to stay in the present. As if sensing Tom's tenuous hold on control, Randy took a step back but couldn't resist getting in the last word. "You'll be hearing from me, Jackie."

Without looking back, he hurried down the path toward the parking lot. Tom flinched as a pair of hands ran up his biceps. Jackie's eyes were round when he met them, but he was grateful not to see any fear in them. Only concern.

The grim beast of rage that lived within him sat back on its haunches, once again leashed. For the time being. He didn't like recognizing that part of him still lingered from his combat days, but if it meant he was able to protect the people he loved, he wasn't above exploiting it.

The remaining parents dispersed as their children joined them.

"Mommy! Tom-tom!" Abby ran over, her face beaming.

Jackie whirled, crouched, and extended her arms, catching her daughter in a tight hug. "Hi! How was school today, sweetie?"

"Good." She gave Tom a hug, her small arms barely able to wrap around his waist. "Hi, Tom-tom."

"Hey, Sprout." He gave her a cuddle. He would do anything for this little girl or her mother. "Let's get going. There's a Christmas cookie at home with your name on it."

"I love Christmas!" Abby exclaimed.

"Me too. Here, let me get that for you." He took the small unicorn backpack from her and draped an arm around her mother's shoulders.

Jackie leaned into him for a split second before stepping back. "You two go ahead. I'd like to talk to your teacher for a moment, Abby."

She rolled her eyes. "Mo-om."

"What? It's a mother's duty to embarrass her daughter, didn't you know that?" She winked then jogged toward the doors before they closed. "Miss Clarissa? Can I have a minute?"

Tom shook his head. Jackie had mastered the art of putting on a bright face. Despite being shaken up, nobody looking at her would know it. Sometimes, it concerned him how easily she wore that mask.

Abby climbed up into her car seat and waited for him to fasten her seat belt. "Miss Clarissa says there are only three more days until Christmas vacation! Francis said her family is going to Colorado to see her grandma."

"That sounds like fun." He shut the door and made a funny face in the window. Abby giggled and stuck her tongue out at him.

He climbed into the driver's seat and adjusted the heater. "Are you warm enough?"

"Uh-huh." She swung her legs, kicking her feet against the back of the seat. "How far is Colorado?"

"It's far enough away that she'll have to fly on an airplane to get there."

"Wow!" Tom glanced in his rearview mirror and watched as she tilted her head skyward to stare out the window. "I've never been on a plane before."

"Maybe one day."

Jackie rushed down the front walk and jumped in beside him.

"Everything all right?" he asked.

"Hm? It's fine. I wanted to make sure she was aware of the situation and to keep an eye out." It looked like she wanted to say more but thought better of it. Instead, she looked back at her daughter. "Tell me all about your day."

Tom grinned when Abby launched into a story about how she and Francis had started kitty-training school during recess and that they had taken turns being either the kitty or the trainer.

They were nearly home when she asked, "Can we go see Santa? Francis says he's coming to collect our Christmas lists tomorrow. If we miss him, he won't know what to get us!"

"I'm not so sure about that. Besides, Santa has helpers everywhere. He'll be able to figure out what you want," Jackie hedged.

"True, but I'm sure we can pay him a visit tomorrow, just in case." Tom reached over, threading his fingers through hers. He knew she was concerned and still feeling embarrassed. Despite her friendly demeanor, she was intensely private about her personal life. He suspected this wouldn't be the last time Randy showed up trying to make a scene, and he didn't like thinking of her going through this again.

Tom mulled over his plans for the next day and realized he'd have to wake up early to get his weekly supply order completed since he'd taken the afternoon off. Ordinarily, he'd go in tonight, but with Randy lurking around, he didn't feel comfortable leaving them home by themselves. His lips thinned. Not even in town for a full week and the asshole was forcing them to change their routines.

"What?" Jackie asked, looking over at him.

"Nothing."

"I'm sorry." She wrung her hands.

"You have nothing to be sorry about."

"I know, but…"

"But, nothing. Whatever ends up happening, we'll work through it." He squeezed her hand, trying to infuse her with confidence. "Together."

CHAPTER SIX

OTHER THAN TOM waking up and heading to the café early, the next day was like any normal day. Which, in Jackie's opinion, was almost worse. It would be easier to prepare for a constant onslaught of Randy rather than having him show up unexpectedly. By the time she said goodbye to the last customers and locked the door, she was a walking ball of nerves.

She took an extra second to scan the street outside before letting out a sigh of relief.

Fiona came up to stand beside her. "Hey, hon. Olivia told me what's going on. What can I do to help?"

Jackie shook her head. "Honestly, we can't do much. The court date is set for after the holidays. I have an appointment with a family lawyer tomorrow afternoon. I might need to get a few character witnesses, but I'll know more once we meet."

"Sign me up. Whatever will help."

Jackie gave her a hug. "Thanks. What would I do without you and your sisters?"

"Luckily, you won't have to find out." Fiona went back to wiping down tables. "That reminds me. We're having a girls' night out tomorrow. You, me, Livvy, Liz, and Mason's sister, Melody." Jackie opened her mouth but was cut off. "And no excuses! Tom's already agreed to it and has signed up for babysitting duty."

"Your family can be pretty pushy. Anybody ever tell you that?"

Fiona giggled. "All the time, but you're still going."

"Fine." She pretended to pout but was grateful to have such good friends.

*

"Ho! Ho! Ho!" the jolly man in the red suit called out. All the kids standing in line giggled and squirmed as they waited to sit on his lap and tell him what they wanted.

Abby stood on her toes, craning her neck to see what was happening toward the front. "How much longer?" Her voice had raised an octave over the last thirty minutes, taking on a specific whining quality that set Jackie's teeth on edge.

"Not much longer, sweetie," Jackie said, trying to comfort her. "Do you see all the kids that are here to see him? How many elves does it take to make all these toys?"

"I don't know," Abby answered, her voice keeping its impatient edge. "I want to see Santa!"

"Why don't you ladies take a walk around and I'll stay here in line?" Tom suggested.

She shot him a grateful look. "Are you sure you don't mind?"

"Not at all. If you stay in the area, I'll call you when I get close to the front of the line."

"Thank you." Jackie directed her daughter to the right. "Abby, let's go check out the Build-A-Bear store and see if we can find a gift for Francis."

"Okay!"

The brightly colored store was packed. Kids ran back and forth between the various displays of outfits and stuffed animals. Sales clerks attended harried parents searching for the perfect gift. It was a madhouse. Of course, Abby was enthralled.

"Look, a kitty!" She ran to an arrangement of cats in all sizes. "Mom, can I get one?"

Jackie regarded her daughter's bright, shining face. "They are pretty cute," she agreed, "but remember, we're here to find a gift for your friend. Let's pick out something Francis would like."

Abby's expression folded into a pout, but it didn't take long for her to recover. "What if we both got kitties, and they could be best friends and we could play with them together?"

"I guess we'll have to see if Santa gets you one, too."

Abby rolled her eyes and huffed out a sigh, but sensing that her mom wasn't going to cave on the matter, she conceded. "I'll make sure to add it to my Christmas list when I talk to Santa."

"Good idea," Jackie reassured her. "Now, which one of these should we get as a gift?"

After they selected the animal, they watched a machine fill it full of stuffing—a process Abby was mesmerized by. Next, they combed through the racks for the perfect outfit. Jackie was surprised when her daughter selected a rainbow-colored tutu with sparkles and a black leather jacket.

"That's quite a get-up. How did you come up with this combination?"

Abby grinned. "Auntie Fiona told me that girls can be tough and colorful and pretty all at the same time, so that's what this outfit is."

Jackie crouched and gave her daughter a hug, then regarded the newly completed stuffed animal. "It looks like you got it exactly right. Auntie Fi would be very impressed with your choices."

Her phone vibrated in her front pocket, interrupting anything else she might have said. "Hello?"

"You ladies should probably head back. The line is moving, and there are only a few families ahead of us." Tom's voice sounded like dark chocolate over the phone. How could he be so sweet and still manage to sound that sinful?

"Oh, good. We're about to pay, and then we'll make our way over." She hung up as the line moved. Taking a step forward, she said, "Won't your friend love this?" She looked down, but Abby wasn't standing by her hip. "Abby?"

Her heart jumped. She scanned the area around her, frantically searching for her daughter's crown of golden hair.

"Abby!" The mother behind her jumped at her raised voice and drew her own child closer. "I'm sorry, did you see a blonde little girl who was standing right here?"

She shook her head. "Sorry, no. I'm lucky I found the end of the line in this chaos."

Jackie struggled to swallow around the lump in her throat. "Abby? Abby!"

She approached another customer standing near her. "I can't find my daughter. She was standing in line with me, and then she was gone." Frightful suspicions swirled through her mind. What if Randy had somehow gotten hold of her and taken her while she was on the phone?

The woman gave her a concerned look. "What's her name? How old is she?"

"Her name is Abby and she's six." Jackie choked on that last word. Six was such a young age. *Please, don't let anything bad happen to her.*

"Why don't you keep looking around the store? I'll try to inform the clerks that there's a missing a child."

A missing a child. All of her worst nightmares threatened to overwhelm her. Instead, she thanked her and continued walking through the various sections she and Abby had recently been through. "Abby!"

All around her, families were laughing and talking, each blissfully oblivious to the stress building in Jackie's chest. A flash of blonde caught her eye in front of the stuffing machine. The little girl was standing next to an older man wearing a red felt Santa hat. A crowd of kids and adults watched as the machine filled the various stuffed animals.

"Excuse me." She threaded her way through the people. "Excuse me, sorry."

A young woman with a toddler on her hip asked, "Can't you let the kids get a good view?"

Despite her snide tone, Jackie apologized to the other mother. "I'm looking for my daughter. She may be up at the front."

Ducking between another set of kids, she reached her hand out, tapping the shoulder of the little girl. "Mommy! Look! Isn't that stuffed puppy adorable?"

Relief and joy swept through her system and quickly transformed into a wash of anger. "Abigail Louise! *What have I told you about running off like that?*" She removed Abby from the crowd, crouching to hold both of her daughter's shoulders, forcing her to look directly at her. "You nearly gave me a heart attack! Do you have any idea how worried I was?"

Tears shimmered as Abby's smile melted. Her chin quivered. "I only wanted to watch the machine stuff the toys."

"I understand that, but you can't take off without telling me where you are going. We've talked about this!" Jackie scanned the crowd around the machine. "Were you talking to someone else, sweetie?"

Abby looked down at her feet. "No."

"Are you sure?" Again, a familiarity about the man in the hat troubled her.

Her daughter shook her head but refused to look up. She looked contrite enough that Jackie decided to give her a break. "Don't do that again, do you hear me?" Abby nodded. "Okay, then, come on. Tom called and it's time to go meet Santa."

She held her daughter's hand firmly and headed out of the store, but the security system blared when she crossed the threshold. Instantly, a salesclerk materialized. Amazing how fast they appeared now that she'd found her daughter. "Sorry, I forgot I was carrying this. Can you hold it for us?" She gave her name to the salesclerk and promised they'd be back after photos with Santa.

"I was afraid we were going to miss our turn," Tom said when they approached.

Jackie ran a hand through her hair. "Sorry."

They got in line right as a pretty, young brunette in an elf costume came up. "Are you ready to see Santa?" she asked Abby.

Abby, who had been excited all night leading up to this moment, ducked behind Jackie. "Mommy, can you come with me?"

"Sure, honey. Do you know what you'd like to ask for?"

"I have a list." Abby took her hand.

"You do? Then we should definitely let him know." They walked up to the big man, but when it came time to sit on his lap, Abby balked once again. "I don't want to sit on his lap! I want to go home."

Jackie's heart sank. "Sweetie, remember, you told us you wanted to take Christmas photos with Santa? Here he is!"

She shook her head. "This isn't Santa. I don't want to do this anymore. Mommy, please don't make me do this." Her cheeks reddened, and her whole body shook as she started to cry in earnest.

"Honey, of course, you don't have to take a photo. Do you want to watch some of the other kids talk to Santa and see if you change your mind?"

Abby stamped her foot. "I'm not going to change my mind!"

What on earth had gotten into her? Jackie took a deep breath and tried not to show her irritation.

Tom got down to the same level as Abby, his calming presence arresting the brewing tantrum. "I want you to look at me," he said, his deep voice filled with authority.

Abby's pale blue eyes met his, tears suspended on her lashes.

Tom continued. "You don't have to take a photo with Santa if you don't want to. However, there is no reason to talk to your mother like that. Do you understand?"

She looked at her feet. "Yes, Tom."

"Good girl." He ruffled her hair and gave her a grin. "Tell me, what makes you think this isn't the real Santa?"

"Because I met him. He told me that if I did what he said, that he would take me on a trip with him." She threw her arms around

Tom. "But I don't want to go with him. I want to stay right here with you and Mommy!"

"What?" Jackie and Tom looked at each other with confusion and concern.

Tom lifted her up in his arms. "When did this happen?"

She gestured back toward the Build-A-Bear. "At the toy store."

Jackie was dumbfounded. By the time she'd located Abby, she was frantic. She'd hardly noticed anybody else except the man standing next to her. Had he looked like Santa? All she remembered was a hat and the unsettling feeling of familiarity.

Closing her eyes, she tried to picture the crowd that had been standing around the machine. It had been comprised mostly of children, with a few adults standing around the edges.

What if someone had lured her away? Were her worst fears beginning to manifest themselves, or was she feeling paranoid because Randy was in town?

The same concern must have crossed Tom's mind, because he said, "You understand that you're not supposed to go anywhere with strangers, right? If someone asks you to go with them, what do you do?"

"I run straight to you or Mommy."

"That's right. And you make sure to tell us what happened."

A look of confusion crossed her face. "But he wasn't a stranger. It was *Santa!*"

Jackie looked at her daughter, trying to figure out how she could have seen another man that looked like Santa. "Even if it is Santa, we want to be told where you are and who you're with. It's better if we all go as a family."

"Okay."

"Excuse me?" The brunette elf was back. "Do you want to take photos with Santa or not? There's a line of people waiting, and we should keep things moving."

Tom bounced Abby in his arms until she giggled. "What do you say, Sprout? How about getting a picture taken with Santa?"

A big guffaw erupted as he swooped her up and down in his arms. "Yes!"

Jackie enjoyed watching the two of them. She was convinced Tom was some kind of child whisperer. Nothing else fully explained how he could talk her daughter off an emotional ledge.

"What are you going to ask for?" Tom inquired.

She whispered in his ear. Whatever she said must have been a doozy, because his expression warmed. He gave her a squeeze and a kiss on top of her head. "Sounds good, Sprout."

She patted him on the shoulder then clambered down out of his arms. She went up to Santa and sat on his lap as if it were the most comfortable thing to do in the world.

"What did she tell you?" Jackie asked out of curiosity.

He shook his head and gave her an enigmatic look, but before he could answer, Abby was waving them over.

The elf walked back over to them. "Did you want a family portrait? It's ten dollars extra."

Tom got his wallet out. "Don't worry, Jackie, I have this."

"Are you sure?"

"Yeah, yeah, go ahead."

He paid the elf and watched Jackie's progress. She made her way over to Santa and her daughter but stood to one side, uncomfortable with the idea of sitting on his lap.

"Come here, Tom-tom!"

Tom hesitated. "You and your mom should probably—"

"Tom," Jackie said, gesturing toward him, "please join us. I'd love to have a photo of the three of us together."

One of the young elves rushed forward, took Tom's arm, and directed him to stand slightly behind Jackie. Tom placed a hand upon Jackie's waist, she rested a hand on Santa's right shoulder, and Abby sat in Santa's lap, grinning ear to ear.

CHAPTER SEVEN

"YOU DIDN'T!" OLIVIA gasped. "You actually slapped him? In front of everybody?"

Jackie took another sip of wine, a little embarrassed now that she'd had a chance to calm down from yesterday's incident. "I was irate! Honestly, I don't even remember raising my hand."

Liz leaned forward and gave her a high five. "Yes! Sounds like he got off easy."

"That's how I felt." Jackie grew quiet, remembering Randy's response. "Unfortunately, the consequences might have me regretting it."

"He deserved it and more," Fiona insisted. "Besides, it sounds like there are plenty of witnesses who would be able to testify he touched you first."

"I didn't think of that, but you're right. Amy would probably vouch for me." She rubbed her temple before dropping her head into her hands. "I still haven't figured out how I'm going to introduce him to Abby."

"Are you sure it's going to come to that?" Melody asked, sounding concerned.

Jackie raised her head. "No, but it looks likely."

Liz snorted out a sound of disgust. "I still can't believe he randomly showed up and decided he wanted to be a dad after all this time. There has to be a catch."

"Mason is looking into it, but investigating without a warrant means he's limited in what he can do," Olivia explained before popping an olive into her mouth. "Although, I'm wondering if this incident would give him just cause. I'll have to ask him when I get home tonight."

The five of them had taken over one of the booths at Olivia's restaurant, Eclipse. A platter of bruschetta drizzled in olive oil and a balsamic reduction and a deluxe charcuterie board filled with aged pepperoni and dried salami, a variety of gourmet cheeses, olives, and roasted red peppers sat in the middle of the table.

When she'd been invited—or rather informed that she was having a girls' night—out with the sisters and Melody, Jackie had been hesitant. Ever since finding out Randy was in town, she'd felt a driving urge to stay close to Abby.

The only reason she was sitting and drinking wine with them now was because Tom was watching Abby. She'd left them in the kitchen making homemade pizzas a little over an hour ago.

"How is Tom doing with all of this?" Fiona asked.

Jackie sighed. "So far, he's managed to keep his cool. Better than me, anyway." She shot them a rueful grin. "I get the feeling he's hanging on to his control by a thread, though. If he does lose it, Randy's in for a hell of a lot more than a slap in the face."

"Let's hope it doesn't come to that," Olivia said. Jackie knew that Olivia was the only other person who had seen Tom's capacity for violence. She thought back to the day when Olivia, Mason, Tom and herself had stood on the sidewalk, looking at the burnt-out ruins of the Three Sisters Café.

Tom had threatened to kill Olivia's stalker if he dared to hurt her. Jackie could tell he hadn't been joking when she'd seen the banked rage cross his face. That had been the first time she'd fully understood what he was capable of doing, what he'd probably had to do to survive when he was a soldier in Afghanistan.

Before that, she'd had a general idea of the lengths he'd be willing to go to in order to keep her and Abby safe. Most of the time, if she were being honest with herself, the memory of him threatening to kill Olivia's stalker made her feel safe and cared for. Mainly because she never believed the situation would ever get that extreme.

"I'm worried that he's going to do something stupid now that Randy is filing for joint custody," Jackie confessed. "He's wound up tight, and all it's going to take is one wrong move on Randy's part."

"Which, judging by what you've told us, seems like a distinct possibility," Liz said.

Jackie's lips twisted. "Exactly."

"You could try filing a restraining order on him. At least until the hearing in January," Olivia suggested.

"That's not a bad idea," Jackie said. "We should ask Mason if that would be possible."

"That reminds me," Fiona interjected. "How did your meeting with the family lawyer go?"

"Not bad. I got the impression that Jen Serres is not a woman you mess around with." Jackie shivered. "I'm glad she's on my side."

"Good! Sounds like you're going to need someone like that," Liz said.

Becky, a young waitress who used to work at the Three Sister's Café, came up to their table. "Hello, I wanted to check on everybody. Is there anything else you'd like tonight?"

Olivia beamed. "Maybe another round of wine, ladies? In fact, why don't you bring a fresh bottle?" She assured the other women, "Don't worry. Mason agreed to drive us home, which means we can relax and drink up."

"One bottle of wine. Would you like anything else?" Becky asked.

Olivia perked up. "Do we still have some of that chocolate peppermint torte?" When Becky confirmed that they did, Olivia's eyes widened. "Ooh! Bring a couple slices of that, too, please. With five forks for sharing. Anybody want anything else?"

"Nope, that sounds perfect." Fiona flung an arm around her sister's shoulders as their waitress ran off to complete the order. "Have I told you how great it is to have a sister who owns the nicest restaurant in town?"

Liz raised her glass. "Hear! Hear!"

"Unfortunately, I don't take advantage of that fact nearly enough." Olivia raised her voice with her glass. "To good friends and girls' night out!"

"I'll drink to that. Cheers!" Jackie said.

It was another two hours before the women were ready to take off.

"Ugh, I'm not going to be able to eat again for at least a few days!" Fiona eyed the last bite of torte on her fork before popping it into her mouth.

Liz rubbed her stomach. "Me neither."

"That dessert was amazing," Jackie told Olivia. "Is that a new menu item?"

"It is. I added it to the specials menu for the holiday. It's been our bestseller."

"I can see why!" Melody said. "Considering my bed-and-breakfast is only a few steps away, it's a dangerous temptation."

"Please, as if you have anything to worry about." Olivia smiled warmly at her friend. "I found the recipe online but couldn't resist putting my own spin on it." Her phone vibrated. "Looks like Mason is pulling into the parking lot. Is everybody ready to go?"

"Absolutely! Get me away from here before I eat anything else," Fiona said.

The women climbed out of the booth.

"You ladies go ahead," Olivia instructed. "I'm going to take care of Becky."

"Are you sure you don't want us to? You picked up the tab, after all," Liz asked.

"No, no, I got it. Tell Mason I'll be out in a minute, would you?"

"Sure," Liz said.

The air was cold enough to sting as they stepped into the night. Jackie huddled deeper into her coat, wishing she'd remembered to wear a scarf.

"Brrr," Fiona exclaimed, stomping her feet. "Is it supposed to snow tonight?"

Liz shook her head. "Not tonight, but later this week it might. Gonna have to make sure the tow truck is ready."

"Thank you for the company, ladies! I'm going to head back to the house." Melody waved to her brother in the driver's seat, gave each of them a hug, and began walking back to La Luna Vista. Jackie admired the way the bed-and-breakfast sparkled and glowed with Christmas lights. Melody had such a good eye for decorating.

The three women trudged to the SUV, where Mason was waiting for them, and squeezed into the backseat.

"Hello!" Fiona said.

He rotated in his seat. "Ladies. Did you have a good night?"

"Hell yeah, we did," Liz said.

Jackie agreed. "It was long overdue. Thank you for driving us."

"My pleasure. I hope it relieved some of the stress you've been under. I take it Olivia is attending to business?" She stepped out of the restaurant. "There she is."

Olivia hurried across the parking lot and climbed into the front seat. "Hi." She gave him a kiss. "Thanks for playing chauffeur tonight."

He brushed a hand over her cheek. "At your service. It's cold out here. Let's get you ladies home. Jackie, you're first."

As she sat sandwiched between Fiona and the door, Jackie felt warm and comforted by the presence of her friends. It was hard to imagine anything truly bad happening when she'd built up such a great community of people around her.

She reminded herself of that fact when she waved goodbye from her front step and watched them drive away.

*

Inside, the house was quiet. "Hello?" she whispered while placing her bag on the bench by the door. The kitchen was spotless; even the dishes in the dry rack had been put away. The smell of garlic and tomato sauce still lingered in the air, which would have been tempting if she hadn't eaten such a good meal at the restaurant.

Halfway down the hallway, she saw a soft glow from the crack beneath her daughter's bedroom door. Quietly, she turned the doorknob and poked her head in.

The view made her heart melt. Abby was snuggled around her favorite stuffed animal, a bunny named Chicken that she'd had since she was born. Tom lay beside her, a favorite children's book lying open in his lap, her daughter's shoulders cradled under his arm. A bedside lamp bathed them in amber light.

She wanted to take a mental picture of this moment, to remember the utter sense of peace she felt when looking at them.

Tom woke. His eyes glittered like black coal, startling her out of her reverie. "Sorry," she whispered. "I didn't mean to disturb you."

Warmth emanated from his gaze. Glancing down at the little girl tucked into his side, he took a deep breath before slowly easing his arm out from under her head. She sighed then rolled over with her bunny.

With great care, he stood and tucked the duvet up around her shoulders. A soft smile graced his face while he stared down at her. Jackie backed out into the hallway as he flicked the light off and closed the door, leaving it cracked open a couple of inches.

"I must have dozed off. How was…?"

Jackie smoothed her hands up over his chest, wrapped her arms around his neck, and brushed a warm, lingering kiss across his lips.

He moved in, pressing her body up against the wall, and claimed her. Devoured her. Consumed her.

Firm hands gripped her ass, lifting her until she could wrap her legs around his waist. She ground her hot center against his hard length, reveling in the friction between them. A few steps later and the world shifted. She found herself deposited on the bed. Tom followed, his body a delicious weight on hers.

She would never get enough of this man.

Strong fingers combed through her hair before he gripped her scalp, raising her mouth to meet his once again. Their tongues tangled. Sampling, savoring, nipping, and teasing each other, building the tension and anticipation between them. His need grew and he ground his hips against her.

He raised himself on his forearms and looked down at her. The heat of his hand seeped through her dress as he cupped her breast. She arched her back as he squeezed his fingers.

His groan was throaty with desire. "Let's get you out of your clothes." He stood and helped her off the bed. "Turn around."

Jackie did as he instructed. His fingers skated along the sensitive skin of her neck when he brushed her hair aside. Slowly, he unzipped the back of her dress, leaving her exposed. Cool air and anticipation had her nerves zinging along her skin.

He traced one finger down her spine, slipping the dress off her shoulders. It fell to her hips and got caught on her curves. Deftly, he undid her bra and dispatched it unceremoniously to the floor before reaching around and filling his hands with her breasts.

Her head fell back to rest on his shoulder while he plucked her sensitive nipples. Hot breath traced the pulse at the base of her neck as he pressed kisses into her flesh.

"I love the way you respond to me," he growled in her ear.

She stepped back and faced him so he could watch her push her dress down and was rewarded by his quick inhalation when her garter belt and stockings were revealed. "Holy shit, woman." Still wearing her heels, she stepped out of the fabric puddled at her feet to let him get a good look at her.

His reaction empowered her. Emboldened her.

"No panties? You mean to tell me you were having a girls' night looking like this under your clothes?" He stalked toward her. "You're lucky I don't tie you up to a bedpost for a week."

Picking her up by the waist, he laid her down on the bed behind her, lifting her feet onto the mattress.

"Tom?" Her voice quivered with yearning.

He knelt on the floor in front of her, spreading her legs wide.

"I love the way you get wet for me." A whimper escaped her when he leaned forward, his breath scalding her sensitive flesh. Flattening his tongue, he took one long, slow lick, finishing with a flick of his tongue on her sensitive nub. "Your passion tastes sweet and creamy, like white chocolate."

Her hips rose of their own volition as she chased her pleasure, but he gripped her tighter, holding her still as he repeated the motion over and over again.

Her head thrashed from side to side as she was subjected to his sweet, torturous tongue-lashings, each stroke setting her on fire until she was melting and burning at the same time.

Jackie clenched the comforter beneath her, holding on with everything she had. Each thrust and stroke of his tongue left her panting and begging for release until she was sure she couldn't take any more... but she did.

*

Tom fluttered his tongue where he knew she wanted it most, plunged two fingers into her hot, wet depths, then watched as she exploded with pleasure. Her legs were a vise around his head, his whiskers scraping against her silken thighs.

Her breathy cries echoed in his mind as she drifted down from her climax. He loved the way her skin flushed with desire, her breasts peaked and a deep rosy hue. He stood, gazing down at her limp limbs and satiated body with male pride.

Her blonde hair, usually polished and sleek, was a wild cloud against the bedspread. Deep blue eyes fluttered as she pinned him with a satisfied look. "Wow."

Following her attention as it dipped lower, he watched as she took in the way his cock strained against the sweatpants he'd changed into earlier that evening. She braced herself on her elbows, her legs still splayed before him. Biting her lip, she said, "Take your clothes off." Her voice was husky, still raw from her climax. He ripped his T-shirt off then jerked his pants down, letting them fall to the floor.

He was gratified by the way she ogled his body with raw female appreciation. When she licked her lips, his erection jumped and bobbed like a witching rod toward water. Sitting up, she grasped him with one hand, her mouth open and inches from his weeping tip. It took all of his self-control to keep his clenched fists by his sides and let her take the lead.

He groaned as her hot breath sent a riot of sensations skittering down the length of his body. The expression she gave him was seductive and secretive like she knew exactly what she was doing to him and enjoyed torturing him with the same brand of pleasure he'd used on her.

Looking up at him from beneath heavy lids, she teased him, barely letting his tip enter her plush mouth. The smooth skin along the inside of her lips felt like heated satin when they eventually wrapped more firmly around him. Gradually, she slid him in deeper, never breaking eye contact. Watching himself sink into her warm, wet, willing mouth was nearly enough to unravel him. His hips bucked convulsively forward, but one of her hands had a firm grasp on the base of his shaft and the other gripped his ass. He could feel the bite of her nails as they dug into his flesh, asserting her control.

"Fuuuuccckkk." He wanted to drop his head back, but the intensity of her gaze possessed him. His fingers threaded through her hair as if they had a mind of their own. The urge to yank her head back and fuck her mouth nearly overwhelmed him.

Her cheeks hollowed slightly as she drew him out, swirling her tongue over his sensitive tip before sliding him fully back in. She hummed appreciatively when he hit the back of her throat, and the vibration sent ripples throughout his system.

Over and over, she took him in until the pressure and tension built up in his balls and a familiar frisson of electricity began to climb from the base of his spine. As tempting as it was to finish with her lips wrapped around him, he was desperate to prolong the moment. He gently yanked her hair, and she released him with a pop. Her whine of protest was nearly enough to undo his resolve.

"Not this way," he growled. "I need to be inside you."

The small furrow of consternation between her brows would have been endearing if he hadn't been ridden by passion. He thumbed her full wet lips when she gave him a pout. "I love your mouth, but I want to be able to fully appreciate this getup you're wearing." He stepped back and helped her from the bed, giving her a hot kiss before turning and bending her over the mattress.

With one hand on the small of her back, he pressed her down until her ass was framed perfectly by the garter straps that held up her sheer black stockings. It was a pale, creamy globe in contrast.

Although she was quite a bit shorter than he, her heels placed her entrance at the perfect height to receive him. He ran a finger through her silky desire before inserting it, testing her readiness. She groaned and arched her back, spreading her legs even farther in invitation. He slipped his tip through her juices, circling the edge of her opening. Unable to wait any longer, he gripped her hips and drove into her, seating himself fully.

"Tom!" she cried, and her pleasure fed his own. He dug his fingers into her flesh as he slammed into her body, again and again, each thrust ratcheting their desire to a feverish pitch. Her inner muscles felt like a velvet vise, clutching at him each time he slid out before he crashed back into her.

He couldn't last much longer. Reaching around, he fluttered a finger along her clitoris, which flung her over the edge. Her climax clenched and milked him until he finally let go and filled her with everything he had.

Spent and sweaty, they fell forward onto the bed, his weight pressing her into the mattress. The sound of their panting filled the air as they worked to catch their breath. After another moment, he raised up on his forearms and looked at the woman still sprawled beneath him. Tracing his fingertips along her back, he was rewarded when she shivered with aftershocks.

With a groan, he rolled over and stretched out beside her. Her face was still half-buried in the bedding, but he could see the edge of a cat-that-ate-the-canary grin. "What?" he asked, brushing a strand of hair back behind her ear.

"If that's the reception I get when coming home from a girls' night out," she mumbled, "I should be doing more of those."

"That's the reception you get when you come home in a getup like this." He snapped one of her garters, chuckling when she yelped.

"Hey!" She half-heartedly swatted his hand away.

"I love you."

The laughter died in her throat, and she reached up to stroke his cheek. "I love you, too."

Later that night, after they were both tucked into bed, Tom held her close. Jackie had already drifted off to sleep, and he took comfort in her deep and even breathing. It didn't matter what the DNA said; this was his family and he would fight to defend it—no matter what.

CHAPTER EIGHT

FRIDAY WAS COLD and blustery, with all the forecasts predicting snow later that evening. Trees swayed and shook the last of the lingering leaves from their branches. Everything had faded into browns and grays weeks ago, but Jackie missed the riotous colors of autumn.

She stared out the café window and watched as people scurried along Main Street, eager to get their errands done. Other than a few holdouts lingering over coffee, business was slow. Ordinarily, she'd take the opportunity to restock items, but today she felt particularly unmotivated.

"You've been wiping the same table down for the last five minutes," Fiona observed.

Jackie sighed and focused on her friend. "Has it only been five? I wouldn't be surprised if it was closer to fifteen."

"I was being kind," Fiona said. "Anything you want to talk about?"

She shook her head. "There isn't anything new to report. I haven't seen Randy since the incident at school.

"That's a good thing, isn't it? Did you look into filing that restraining order like we suggested?"

"I haven't had time." She winced when Fiona rolled her eyes. "What? It's true! The holidays are always a little crazy. Besides, I was hoping it wouldn't come to that."

"Well, you got your wish. I mean, as long as Randy isn't harassing you, that's good news."

"I guess." Her attention was caught by the wind as it blew down a sandwich-board sign advertising snow shovels for sale. Moments later, Frank came out of the hardware store and brought it inside. "I'm worried there's a second shoe that's going to drop."

Fiona tilted her head. "We already realize there's a second shoe that's going to drop, in January. It isn't as if he hasn't made his intentions clear about what he plans to do—or what he wants."

A look of doubt crossed Jackie's face as she squinted in consternation. "That's what bothers me. Why is he feeling paternal now when he's never shown any interest before? His reasons for doing this don't ring true to me." She moved to the next table. "I'm afraid there's more to this situation than what we're seeing."

"What else could it be?" Fiona pondered her words. "Couldn't it simply be that he's out of jail and wants a second chance?"

"I don't know." She flung her hands up. "If I understood his motivations, at least I'd be able to predict what his next action will be. Maybe I wouldn't be such a basket case."

"What does Tom have to say about it?"

Shaking her head, Jackie bent down to retrieve the dishtowel she'd accidentally flung out of her hand. "He's equally as concerned as I am, but he's more of the brooding, silent type."

Disapproval and concern laced Fiona's tone. "You two should make sure you're communicating about this. Remember, you're stronger together. Besides, Tom would never let anything happen to either one of you. He loves Abby as if she were his own."

A warm smile replaced the worried look on Jackie's face. "True. Sometimes, I wish she was." Her lips twisted and she shook her head. "But then Abby wouldn't be Abby, and I can't imagine a world without her."

Fiona placed a hand on her arm. "Neither could I." Her expression brightened. "Which reminds me, I can't wait for her recital tonight."

Jackie beamed. "Me neither! Wait until you see her in her elf costume." She laughed. "She's utterly adorable."

"Olivia said she wanted to arrive early, which means we'll probably show up a little after four."

"Great, but don't be surprised if I press you into service for the bake sale. Half the mothers wind up chasing after their kids or scrambling to get their costumes put together and forget they're supposed to be selling."

"I am at your service. Whatever I can do to help," she assured her. A jingle from the front door rang out as a new customer entered the café. "Looks like our reprieve is over." Fiona strode toward the hostess station. "Mrs. Crowley and Mr. Harrison, I'm surprised you braved the wind and cold today."

"Pfft, what's a little wind at our age?" Mrs. Crowley straightened her shoulders. "Us New Englanders are made of sturdier stock than that!"

Mr. Harrison patted her hand that was threaded through his arm. "We certainly are. How are you doing, dear?"

"I haven't finished my holiday shopping yet, but otherwise, I'm doing well," Fiona answered. "Your usual booth, I'm assuming?"

"Perfect," Mrs. Crowley said with approval. "Does Tom have any of his clam chowder today? I feel like soup."

Jackie waved to the elderly couple before heading to the back. She should take this opportunity to start restocking inventory.

*

A woman with an open and friendly face walked into the school cafeteria, precariously balancing three boxes. "Hi, Jackie. Where would you like me to put these?"

"Laura, I'm glad you're here." Jackie took the top box, surprised by its weight. "Wow! How many did you make?"

"Oh, it's only three dozen," Laura dismissed. "I wanted to make sure there was a variety."

"That's great, thank you! Everybody always asks for your delicious cupcakes. I can't wait to see your Christmas designs." She looked at the handful of white tables that had been set up. "Why don't we put them front and center?"

Laura set the boxes down. "I'll get the stand from my car and start setting up."

"Perfect." Jackie greeted the next mom who had arrived. "Sugar cookies! Those look delicious, Janna."

"I had a late-night surgery last night. I hope it's okay that they're store-bought."

"That's no problem at all. I hope your patient is doing well?"

"She'll have a few weeks of recovery, but I'm happy to report that Herb's cat, Nutmeg, is resting peacefully. I'll probably have to leave early to check on her."

"A veterinarian's work is never done. I hope she heals quickly." She gestured to an open space. "Why don't you place your cookies over there?"

"We're here! Where do you want us?" Olivia said as she, Mason, and Fiona arrived. "I brought some of the Christmas cookies we made the other day."

"Fantastic. Olivia, can you put them in with mine?" She gave them all a hug. "I'm happy you made it. Abby couldn't stop talking about how excited she was. Isn't Liz coming?"

"Yes, but she called and said they're running late," Olivia confirmed.

"I'll keep an eye out for them. Fiona, can you take the cash box and set up down at the end of the tables? Olivia, if you would start putting prices on all of this stuff. Use your discretion, but nothing over five dollars. Mason, why don't you head to the auditorium and reserve a few more chairs? You'll find our coats are in the second row on the right."

"On it," Mason said before heading to the double doors.

Fiona wandered over to the place Jackie had indicated. Olivia lingered before starting to price the baked goods. "Any sign of you-know-who?"

Jackie brushed an errant strand of hair from her forehead. "No, thank goodness, but I've been on pins and needles keeping an eye out for him."

"Where's Tom?"

"He took Abby backstage to meet up with her class. He's hesitant to let her out of his sight."

Olivia sighed. "I hate that you two are having to deal with this—and during the holidays, no less!"

"That's exactly how I feel. I hope she doesn't catch on to what's happening. Thankfully, we've managed to keep her insulated from it."

"At least, there's that," Olivia agreed. "It looks like people are starting to filter in. I better get to pricing all this yummy goodness."

"I appreciate it," Jackie said as another parent came up to her with questions.

By the time the recital was ready to start, most of the items were sold and everybody had moved into the auditorium. Fiona returned the cash box before going to find her seat. Jackie consolidated the remaining treats and cleaned the empty tables before slipping down the darkened aisle toward the front.

She waved at Liz and Alex seated at the end of the row, then sank into her seat right as Principal Johnson finished his welcoming speech.

"How did it go?" Tom whispered.

"We did well! Thankfully, we sold enough to finish funding the school garden this spring."

"Congratulations." He threaded his fingers through hers before returning his attention to the stage.

The evening was full of joy as each grade showcased the performances they'd been working on. The school choir sang a number of holiday classics, and the band only made Jackie cringe a handful of times.

The best part was watching Abby up on stage with bells in hand, ringing her little heart out. Jackie's heart burst with pride as she beheld the joy on her daughter's face. The whole group of friends agreed she was the cutest elf up there.

When the lights came up, a crowd of parents filled the aisles and everybody jockeyed toward backstage to retrieve their children.

"I better find Amy and give her the proceeds from the bake sale. Thank goodness I'm not the PTA president! I don't know how she does it," Jackie said.

"I can't imagine," Olivia said.

"Why don't you guys head out, and I'll meet you by the front doors?" Jackie suggested.

Fiona nodded. "Okay, can we get some hot chocolate afterward?"

"What a perfect idea!" Jackie craned her neck and spotted Amy across the auditorium. "Oh, there she is. Tom, will you retrieve Abby?" She pressed a quick kiss to his cheek.

"Sounds good." He cut a wake through the other parents, heading toward the backstage area, while she continued on her own mission.

Crossing the room wasn't a fast or easy process, because every few steps parents stopped her to talk. Ordinarily, she enjoyed the friendly, social atmosphere, but tonight was different. Maybe she felt that way because she knew Randy was in town, or perhaps it was because of the stress from coordinating the bake sale, but she'd been suffering from low-grade anxiety all evening and couldn't shake her unease. A ball crouched in her stomach, and the pressure behind her eyes was enough to make her want to skip the hot chocolate and reach for a glass of wine, instead.

Thankfully, Amy met her halfway. "Hi, Jackie! Your daughter was utterly adorable up on that stage."

"Thanks, I agree. Matthew sounded amazing during his solo. He has quite a good voice."

"Thank you. I'll tell him you said that. He practiced nonstop at home." She rolled eyes in good humor.

Jackie cracked up. "Trust me, I get it. Be thankful he wasn't also playing the jingle bells." They chuckled in commiseration. "At any rate, I wanted to make sure you got this before we take off tonight." She handed Amy the cash box.

"I appreciate you doing all the work for the bake sale this year." She rubbed her large bump. "This last trimester has kept me exhausted. I honestly couldn't have handled it."

"Truly, it wasn't a problem." She glanced across the room. "Anyway, I'm gonna go get my daughter. Have a good night."

Jackie quickly spotted her friends. "Hey, guys. Tom and Abby aren't here yet?"

"We haven't seen them," Fiona said.

"Hold on, this is Tom calling," Mason said, before answering the phone. "Hello? What's up?" He looked up at Jackie. "No shit? Be right there."

As he hung up, the feeling of dread that had been haunting Jackie all evening came on in full force. "What's wrong?"

"You better come with me. We'll be right back." Mason took her elbow and steered her through the remaining families who were still chatting in the lobby. He headed down the hallway toward the backstage door.

"No! Leave me alone! You are not my daddy!"

At Abby's plaintive cry, Jackie yanked out of Mason's grasp. The linoleum tiles squeaked beneath her shoes as she sprinted down the hallway and rounded the corner.

What she saw stopped her heart.

Randy was trying to talk to her as tears ran unchecked down Abby's red cheeks. Tom held an arm around Abby and another up to shield her from the other man's advances. His face was a thunderstorm. He was clearly struggling to remain civil in front of the small gathering of parents and children who were attracted by the commotion.

"Step back. Now. This is your last warning," he growled.

"Mommy!" Abby rushed toward her, flinging herself into her arms.

Jackie picked her up. "Shh," she stroked her daughter's hair, "it's going to be okay."

"He says he's my daddy, but I don't want him to be my daddy! He's a big meanie face!" The familiar scent of baby shampoo was comforting as Jackie tucked her daughter into the crook of her neck.

"Randy, you can't come here like this," she chastised.

"You've left me no choice! I demand to see my daughter. If that means I have to crash her school holiday play, then that's what I'm going to do."

"Which, once again, illustrates why you don't deserve to have a relationship with her," Jackie said. "All you're worried about is yourself—what *you* want. Did you ever stop to consider how it would make her feel?"

"I'm so sorry. I heard what was happing and got here as soon as I could," Principal Johnson said before turning toward Randy. "You need to leave these premises immediately."

Randy took a step forward, his brows furrowing. "Or what?"

"Or I'll be forced to cite you for disturbing the peace," Mason said. He propped his hands on his hips, conveniently uncovering the detective badge hanging from his waist.

Randy sneered. "Must be nice to have the cops at your beck and call. This isn't over, Jackie."

"It is for tonight. Go back to where you came from, Randy." She shifted Abby's weight higher up on her hip. "And, in case you start getting any other bright ideas, I am going to document this incident and will be compiling a harassment file. Do yourself a favor and don't bother trying to see us before the court date in January. You'll only make things worse."

A muscle ticked in his clenched jaw, and his face flushed from scarlet to burgundy. "You will regret this." He tried to place a hand on Abby's shoulder, but Tom was there to stop him. "I'll be back, sweetie. Don't you worry."

Jackie's arms tightened around her daughter's trembling body. Mason put a hand on his shoulder, but Randy shook his hand off. "I'm going. I'm going."

Mason looked at her. "Are you two going to be all right?"

She forced her trembling lips into a smile for Abby's sake. "We'll be fine. Thank you, Mason."

"Anytime." He watched Randy's retreating figure. "I'm going to make sure he leaves the building."

Tom shook his hand. "Thanks for having my back."

Mason raised an eyebrow. "Thanks for keeping your cool. I'm not sure I would have been able to practice such self-restraint." He addressed the small group of parents who had lingered during the ordeal. "That's enough excitement for tonight. Why don't you folks take off?"

Most of them began to disperse, but an older woman Jackie had never seen before stepped closer to her. "If thy daughter be shameless, keep her in straightly..." she whispered.

A chill ran down Jackie's spine. "What was that?" But the woman had moved off into the crowd. Others sent Jackie sympathetic looks or patted her on the shoulder as they passed, but nobody else mentioned the eccentric woman.

"How are you feeling?" Tom enveloped them in a big bear hug while the crowd dispersed. "I was seconds away from knocking that guy out, but I wasn't sure how far you wanted me to take it."

Jackie dismissed the woman's odd comment, deciding that in all the excitement, she may have misheard the woman. The last thing she needed was to become paranoid. They had enough on their plate.

"I'm glad you didn't." She inspected Abby's tear-stained cheeks, wiping them with her thumb. "I'm sorry that happened, but you were such a brave little girl. I'm proud of you, sweetie."

She hiccupped. "Was that bad man my daddy?"

Sorrow squeezed Jackie's heart, but lying was not an option. Not when a court date loomed on the near horizon. "Yes, technically, he is, but he went away a long time ago—before you were born—and it takes more than that to be a family. It takes time, effort, caring, and love to become a family."

"Like the way Tom reads me bedtime stories and makes me chocolate chip pancakes and helps me find Chicken when I lose her?"

She met his warm eyes, their depths stormy with emotion. Angst threatened to cut off her voice, but she managed to croak out, "That's right, baby. Exactly like that."

Tom's hug was strong and firm around her shoulders. He bent over and kissed the crown of Abby's head before placing a gentle kiss on Jackie's lips. "Come on. Let's go get some hot chocolate and talk about what a great elf you were."

"Okay!" Jackie was amazed at how easily Abby shook the incident off. She wiggled and Jackie released her, feeling the loss of her warm body in her arms. Tom took Jackie's hand and they followed, enjoying the sight of Abby racing down the hallway.

CHAPTER NINE

"THE NERVE OF that guy," Liz exclaimed. "Can't Jackie file a restraining order against him, Mason?"

He shook his head. "Unfortunately, no. What he's done hasn't constituted legitimate grounds for one."

"That's messed up that she's stuck having to deal with his harassment!" Fiona shook her head.

Liz snorted. "Why am I not surprised? I swear, sometimes it feels like the whole system is rigged against women."

"Are you implying that only men harass women?" Alex asked, one eyebrow raised.

"No," Liz said, swatting his arm, "but we're both aware that women are more often the victim in these types of circumstances. Quit trying to split hairs."

Olivia sighed. "Come on, you two, let's get back to the matter at hand. This is a serious situation."

Now that Jackie was able to sit around the table with her friends, the implications of the situation were fully sinking in. She dropped her head into her hands and groaned. "What am I going to do? I can't have him showing up and disrupting our lives whenever he wants. How is that fair to me or Abby?"

Tom held Abby's hand as they rejoined the group. "The hot chocolates should be ready in a few minutes."

"Mommy, I got extra marshmallows in mine! The man even gave me a big one while I was standing there."

Jackie reached over and helped her daughter into the chair beside her. "He did? Did you say thank you?"

"I did."

"Well, that sounds super special."

"Abby, you were the best jingle-bell ringer on stage tonight," Fiona said. "You looked like you were having a lot of fun."

"And I loved your elf costume," Olivia added.

Abby beamed from all the attention. "Thanks, Mommy made it for me."

Another family from the school sat a few tables down. Their little boy waved. "Hi, Abby!"

"Hello," she said shyly. Jackie said hello to the little boy's parents but noticed they soon lowered their voices and had their heads bent toward each other. She could only imagine what they were saying.

"Everything okay?" Tom asked Jackie while the rest of the group kept Abby occupied talking about what she wanted for Christmas.

"No," Jackie said. "Honestly, I can't believe this situation with Randy is happening."

He stroked her back. "I'm sorry, honey. Let's try to set it aside and enjoy the holidays as best as we can. We'll tackle the court date and everything else as it comes."

"You're right." She continued, "At least there's one good thing."

"What's that?"

"School is officially on break for the holidays. There's no way he can ambush us on campus again."

Tom's brows rose. "That's true."

She sighed. "I shouldn't let it bother me, but I hate that we've attracted such negative attention. It makes me feel self-conscious, like I felt when I was first starting to show and getting ostracized for it by the church. I've worked hard to rebuild my reputation, and I don't want that shi—" she glanced toward her little girl and amended her vocabulary— "jerk ruining it for us."

"About that," Fiona interjected, "if you wanted to take some shifts off in order to stay home with Abby, I'd be happy to pick up a few more hours at the café. Also, Becky was saying she needed to earn some extra money before her classes start next semester. I bet she'd be willing to help out."

"That's not a bad idea, Fiona. Thank you."

"Sure."

Alex stifled a large yawn. "Well, guys, I'm beat. I had to wake up at four-thirty this morning to get to the new build site."

"Damn, that's early," Mason said. "What's the new project you're working on?"

"A remodel of the historic High Point Inn in Scarborough, but the pressure is on because the property is huge and their summer season reopens in May. I have to get my plans finished before the end of this month because we're scheduled to hit the ground running after New Year's."

"Sounds complex but interesting," Tom said. "I've seen that property featured on a few local programs. It's already a gorgeous hotel. Can't wait to see what you do with it."

Alex leaned forward. "I'm excited about the possibilities. We outbid three other firms for the job. The primary challenge is going to be choosing where and how to preserve the building's history while still meeting modern-day aesthetics and safety standards."

Liz draped an arm around his shoulders. "If anybody is up to the task, it's you."

"Thanks, hon." Alex stood. "Abby, thank you for putting on such a wonderful performance tonight."

"Thank you for coming, Uncle Alex!" she chirped.

Liz ruffled her hair before dropping a kiss on her nose. "See you later, Sprout. Or should I call you Elf?"

She giggled. "No, silly. My name is Abby!"

Liz snapped her fingers. "Oh yeah!" She winked at everyone else. "See you all later. Good luck with the situation, Jackie. I'd be happy to flatten any tires." Glancing at Mason shaking his head, she added, "Hypothetically, of course."

Jackie gave her a rueful smirk. "You'll be the first person I talk to."

The rest of the group finished up and headed home. Flurries started to swirl in the headlights as Tom drove her and Abby back to the house. If not for the earlier events with Randy, the day would have been good.

As usual, Tom picked up on her mood and reached over to hold her hand. "Don't worry. We'll get through this."

"I hope so." She glanced into the backseat at her daughter, who was drifting off to sleep. *But at what cost?*

*

Tom woke but didn't move a muscle. It was a trick he learned early on during combat. Jackie had often told him that it was unnerving, but the habit had saved his life before.

Once, he'd been stationed at a remote camp two hours from the nearest Forward Operating Base in Afghanistan, and an infiltrator had overtaken the soldier on guard. The muted sound of the assailant's boots against the sand had alerted Tom to what was happening. His quick assessment and quiet approach had saved the eight other guys in camp that night.

Unfortunately, the guard couldn't survive his throat being slashed. It was one of a handful of deaths that haunted Tom.

He lay still, homing in on what had woken him.

He took stock of his surroundings. Jackie was rolled away from him, curled up and sleeping peacefully. He didn't smell smoke or gas fumes when he took a deep breath.

There.

It was barely audible, but it sounded like the soft click of a door closing. Tom stared at the ceiling and tried to convince himself it was his imagination, but his past combined with the fact he was still on edge from the incident with Randy earlier were too powerful. He wouldn't be able to go back to sleep until he checked the house and assured himself that everything was as it should be.

Resigned, he cautiously climbed out of bed, taking a moment to pull the comforter over Jackie's bare shoulder before sliding his slippers on. He looked at the alarm clock and realized he'd have to be up in half an hour to head to the café. At this point, he should make a pot of coffee and stay up.

The hallway was shadowed, with the faintest light from the moon filtering in from the kitchen and living room beyond. That was odd. Usually, they kept a nightlight on in the bathroom in case Abby got up during the night. He gave a light knock on the door. "Abby? Are you in there?"

The toilet flushed, and she opened the door with a sleepy grin. "Hi, Tom."

She looked precious standing there in her Christmas PJs featuring Frosty the Snowman. Her hair was messy and her eyes were barely open.

"Hey, sweetie. Did you wash your hands?"

"One sec." She washed her hands then wiped them dry on her pajama top.

Tom stifled a chuckle and corralled her back into her bedroom.

"I forgot Chicken!" She pouted.

"Don't worry, I'll get her. You climb into bed, and I'll be back to tuck you in with Chicken."

She crawled up into her bed and slipped under the comforter while Tom retrieved the beloved stuffed bunny. "Here you go. Let's tuck you in, snug as a bug in a rug." He secured the covers around her. "That good?"

She yawned, already drifting to sleep. "Mm-hm. G'night, Tom-tom."

"G'night, Sprout. Sweet dreams."

"Can you leave the door cracked a little bit?"

"Of course. Go back to sleep." He watched as she snuggled deeper under the comforter until all that was visible was the crown of her head, and then he went to the kitchen. This deal with Randy had him jumpy and nervous, and he didn't like it. Not one bit.

CHAPTER TEN

"GOOD MORNING, MOMMY!" Jackie groaned as her daughter launched herself onto the bed. "Wake up!"

"Mmppfff. What time is it?" she asked before rolling over and ducking under the comforter.

"I don't know, but Tom is gone and I'm hungry." That last word ended with a slight wail, and Jackie knew it was only a matter of time before her daughter transformed from a lovable little girl to a hangry wildebeest.

She peeked out from under the covers. "You're Hungry? Nice to meet you, I'm Mommy."

"Mo-om! My name is not Hungry. My name is Abby, and Abby is hungry!"

"Oh, fine!" She quickly sat up and brushed her hair out of her face. "Just you wait, kid. The shoe is gonna be on the other foot when you're a teenager, and I will enjoy my sweet, sweet revenge."

Her daughter's brow wrinkled in confusion. "What shoes? Why are you talking about shoes, Mommy?"

Jackie smirked. "Give it ten years. You'll see."

They entered the kitchen, and Jackie fell in love all over again when she spotted the freshly made pot of coffee. "Hot damn, I love that man."

She poured Abby a bowl of cereal and placed it in front of her, then checked the produce bin in the refrigerator. Looked like they were going to have to do some grocery shopping soon. "Do you want strawberries or banana slices this morning?"

"Banana slices!"

"Banana slices, *please.*"

"Banana slices, please," Abby repeated.

"Get started on your cereal or it will get mushy. I'll get these ready in a jiffy…" *Right after I pour myself a cup of coffee.*

Once they were seated around the small dining room table, happily breaking their fast, Jackie contemplated her plans for the day. "Guess what?"

"What?" Abby said before slurping another bite from her spoon.

"I don't have to go to work today!"

"Yay!"

"Exactly. You and I should get some Christmas shopping done. What do you say?"

Abby's expression deflated. "Shopping?" Her shoulders hunched.

The reaction was not unexpected, but Jackie had been hoping for a better result. "I know, I know… shopping. But don't you want Tom to have a nice Christmas, too?"

She speared a banana slice. "Yeah."

"Well, then, how about this? We go and do a little bit of shopping and try to pick up some presents, and afterward," Jackie leaned forward and wiped a spot of milk off her daughter's chin, "afterward, we can go to the indoor park for a little bit."

"We can?" Abby bounced in her seat. "Okay!"

Jackie raised her eyebrows and shot her daughter a no-nonsense look. "But you have to be good or we won't be able to go. Do you promise?"

"I promise!"

A couple hours later and those two words mocked her. Man, the value of a promise these days, Jackie thought as she called, "Abby! Please don't play hide-and-seek in those racks. Look! You almost ran into that lady!" She offered an apologetic smile to the woman. "Sorry about that."

"You have quite a little hooligan on your hands." She shot Jackie a disapproving look. "'He that spareth his rod hateth his son: but he that loveth him chasteneth him betimes.' In my day, children were better behaved."

"Excuse me?" Jackie said, affronted. The saying brought forth a flood of unwelcome memories of her father saying the same thing before disciplining her for some perceived transgression.

The older woman ignored her and bent toward Abby. "Are you being a good little girl? You know God is watching, right?"

Abby glanced at her mom with a look of confusion. "Um, yes?"

"Honor your mother, like our Lord Jesus Christ teaches."

"Thank you," Jackie said between clenched teeth before snagging Abby's hand and moving away.

"She was weird," Abby said.

"Shh, it's not nice to talk badly about someone," Jackie reminded her daughter, squeezing her hand to soften the blow of her words. She lowered her voice. "But I agree. I promise we're almost done. We have to buy these last few things, then we'll eat lunch and go to the indoor playground."

She ran a hand over Abby's head. "Look! The line isn't too long."

Thank goodness the store appeared to have every employee working the holiday rush. Ten minutes later, the clerk called, "Next customer, please."

"Hi, I'll take these, please." Jackie placed the garments on the counter. "Can you make it a gift receipt, just in case?"

"Of course," the young man said as he began to ring things up.

"Thank you."

She tried to stifle her impatience when he accidentally scanned the same sweater twice.

"Shoot, I have to call a senior cashier to void one of these." He gave her an apologetic grin. "Sorry, this is only my second day."

Inwardly, she sighed but gave him an understanding smile. Thankfully, it only took a moment for the neighboring employee to fix the error.

Jackie swiped her card then glanced down at her daughter. "Abby?" For crying out loud, not again. "*Abby?*" Turning, she caught sight of Abby's feet as she slipped through a bunch of winter coats hanging on a round rack.

"Would you like your receipt with you or in the bag?"

"I'm sorry? Oh, in the bag is fine." She accepted her purchases, smiled at the clerk, and then walked over to the coat section. "Abby, I asked you not to play in the clothes racks."

On the last word, she whipped two coats apart expecting to find her daughter, but the center was empty.

"Abby, where are you?" she called out in a singsong voice. Bending down, she checked to see whether any of the racks had grown legs.

A giggle to her right had her turning her head, but it was another little girl in a stroller. "Abby? Come on, honey. The longer you hide, the longer it'll take for us to go to the playground."

A flutter of unease crossed her mind, but she pushed it aside along with another set of clothes. "This isn't funny anymore, sweetie. Come out, this instant!"

Jackie scanned the entire section, realizing the store had gotten steadily busier since they'd arrived, which was partly why she had wanted to get the shopping done early. "Abigail Louise!" A part of her winced at the sharpness of her tone, but if it got her daughter moving, it was worth it.

Each empty rack she checked piled on to her stress until she was going through the section methodically.

"Excuse me, have you seen a little girl wandering around here?" she asked a shopper.

"Um, no, I'm sorry." The man took a cursory look around, then continued examining a table full of ties.

"Thank you." Jackie sank to her knees and examined the spaces under the racks, hoping she would find her daughter's knees among the fabric.

"What on earth are you doing?" The reproachful tone sent heat rushing into her cheeks.

Jackie scrambled to her feet, dismayed to see the woman from earlier. "My daughter is playing hide-and-seek again, and I can't find her."

She couldn't keep the edge of panic from lacing her voice.

"'But Jesus said, 'Suffer little children, and forbid them not, to come unto me: for of such is the kingdom of heaven'.'" The intense look on the older woman's face caused Jackie to take a step back.

"I'm sorry?" she asked, unsure how to respond.

The woman's expression cleared. It happened so fast that Jackie wondered if she'd imagined it. "I saw her a minute ago over in that direction." She pointed toward the men's section.

"Over there?" At her nod, Jackie thanked her before striding toward the indicated section. It seemed odd that Abby would gravitate toward the suits and ties. After nearly five minutes of fruitlessly searching, breathing had become difficult. Every cell in her body was screaming that something was wrong.

Seriously wrong.

Most of the time, she didn't like making a spectacle, but now all she wanted to do was scream her daughter's name until she had her back in her arms. Instead, she headed toward the checkout counter. "I insist on speaking to a manager immediately."

"Ma'am, you're going to have to wait in line, like all of these other nice folks." The new cashier's patronizing tone made her clench her jaw, especially after the patience she'd extended to him when he made a mistake checking her items out earlier.

"I'm not trying to buy anything. I can't find my daughter."

"Okay, ma'am, if you could wait—"

She slammed her palm on the counter. The loud crack made

the clerk jump and caught the attention of everybody nearby. "I'm not going to wait! What part of 'my daughter is missing' don't you understand! I need help. Right. Now!" Her chest was a tight knot of emotion. A group of shoppers in line began to whisper and comment on the unfolding drama.

"You still haven't found her?" the gentleman from before asked with increased concern. "What does she look like?"

"She's about this tall"—Jackie held her hand halfway down her thigh— "blonde hair, blue eyes. She's wearing red plaid Christmas leggings and a sweater with a Scottie dog wearing a plaid bow." Turning back to the cashier, she pleaded, "Please, where is your manager, or who should I speak to get a missing-child announcement on the PA?"

The senior cashier from before came forward. "Don't worry, ma'am. I've already made a request for the manager to join us. He's on his way."

The Christmas music stopped, and a man's deep voice said, "Attention all employees. We have a Code Adam. I repeat, a Code Adam. Please stand by for more details."

The senior cashier stepped from behind the counter and approached the line. "Hello, everybody. I'm sorry for the inconvenience, but store exits are officially closed until we can find a missing child. All purchases can be made at the designated register by the east entrance. We appreciate your patience and cooperation."

A collective gasp came from the line of customers. A number of them approached Jackie with offers to help look. Quite a few people were already checking under displays and racks throughout the store.

"I'm sure she's fine," the man holding a handful of ties said, trying to console her. "If she were my child, she'd be grounded for a month."

She frowned. "Thanks."

He patted her on the arm. "Good luck."

A portly gentleman in a white button-down shirt and green tie walked up to her. "Are you the woman with a missing child?"

She gulped. Hearing it said aloud brought home how terrible the situation was. "I am."

"My name is Jerry." He offered her a perfunctory handshake. "I'm going to need to get a description of your daughter, including what shoes she's wearing."

"Her shoes?"

"Yes, ma'am. Will you come with me, please?"

"I'd rather keep looking for my daughter."

"Everybody in the store is looking for your daughter. I have another means of searching that may help us."

He led her down a dimly lit hallway with dingy walls, past the bathrooms, and unlocked a nondescript door. Inside was a small room with a bank of tiny black-and-white monitors and a desk crammed into the corner. There was barely enough room for a cabinet and two chairs.

"Sorry for the cramped quarters. We mainly save the glitz and glamour for the retail side."

"That's fine."

He sat down and placed his hands on the keyboard then began asking questions.

She described her daughter's physical features, as well as her adorable snow boots with red stars on them. The memory of her finding them on sale flashed through Jackie's mind, and she struggled to keep her composure.

"I'm sorry. I know this must be hard. How long ago did you last see your daughter?"

"Um, about ten minutes ago?" She gnawed on her bottom lip. Could it already have been that long? "Wait! I was making a purchase and have the receipt in my bag. It would have a timestamp, right?"

"It would."

She fumbled through the clothes she'd purchased and handed him the slip of paper.

"Looks closer to fifteen minutes, although it must feel longer." He checked the clock. "Unless we find her in the next three minutes, we'll contact the police."

Jackie covered her mouth in horror. This couldn't really be happening. Meanwhile, Jerry double-checked the receipt. "You were at cashier station number four..." he muttered as he tapped on the keys. One of the monitors began reversing the feed until an image of her and Abby popped up.

"You must think I'm a terrible mother," she whispered.

He quickly turned away from the screen. "You'd be surprised how often this happens. Usually, it ends up that the kid headed to the toy section. One time, he'd gone to the bathroom without informing his mom. She was furious."

"Furious would be preferable to what I'm feeling at the moment," she admitted.

He focused back on the monitor. "Let's see what we can find out."

Jackie watched as Abby slipped away and crawled into the rack that she'd searched through earlier. Moments later, her daughter exited the other side and slid under the rack beside it. The toes of her little snow boots peeked out from under one of the coats, and Jackie stifled a giggle that quickly morphed into a sob.

Alarm filled Jerry's face when he looked over at her. Jackie pressed a fist to her mouth and shook her head, willing herself to maintain control. "Please, go on."

They watched as Abby moved to another rack and then out of frame. "Hold on... one second." Jerry tapped on a few more keys, and a new angle popped up on the screen. Jackie watched as the odd Bible-quoting woman spoke to Abby and pointed at something. Whatever it was caught her daughter's eye because she skipped across the aisle and back out of view.

"Dammit." It took another second before a new perspective showed up. "Looks like she was trying on hats." An older man wearing a hat and a large winter coat walked up and said something to make her giggle. Jackie watched the interaction with heightened concern. From this angle, they could only see the back of him, but familiarity nagged at her. She tilted her head and racked her brain.

"Ma'am," the manager's voice drew her attention back to the recording. "Whatever he said, she's going with him."

Dread made her stomach drop as Abby took the older man's hand and they walked away. Tears poured down Jackie's face. How many times had she told her daughter not to talk to strangers or walk off with them? Her kindergarten class had done the Stranger Danger Awareness Program last month! "Oh, my God."

For the first time in six years, Jackie started praying.

CHAPTER ELEVEN

THE AFTERNOON WAS a whirlwind. Reality felt distant and distorted as if Jackie was watching the activity through three feet of glass. All she could hear was Abby's voice greeting her earlier: *"Good morning, Mommy!"*

Tears streamed down her face as she clutched Abby's favorite stuffed animal closer. She buried her nose into the soft fur and savored the smell of her daughter's shampoo. Her whole body curled around the toy as if it were a conduit to her little girl.

Half a dozen people filled her living room, their boots thumping on the carpet as they set up phone lines and computers. Mason had stepped into the role of liaison and was coordinating between the police department and the Child Abduction Response Team, or CART. A black detective with sympathetic eyes was sitting beside her on the couch. Olivia had assured Jackie that the detective had been kind and helpful during her ordeal with the stalker. What was her name?

The pressure that had built up in her head had become nearly unbearable. The woman said something, but Jackie didn't catch it. "I'm sorry, what?" she asked. "Could you please repeat that?"

Her first name had started with a *C*... C Something... Jackie pondered it until the memory snapped into place. *That's right, CeCe.*

"You've already told me that you suspect the biological father could be behind all of this. His name is Randy, right?" When Jackie confirmed, CeCe continued. "We are absolutely looking into that angle. In fact, a police car has been dispatched to his apartment, but we can't assume anything at this point. Can you remember anything else that felt odd or out of place?" Officer CeCe set a hand on her shoulder. "I recognize that this is hard, but you must concentrate. Any little detail can help us find your daughter."

Jackie swallowed the sob that crouched in her throat and fought to maintain her sanity. Her whole world had become unending anguish. She kept hoping it was all a dream that she would wake up from.

"Jackie?"

"I—I'm sorry. I've been racking my brain, but I've already told you everything I can remember."

"Don't worry. You're doing great," she soothed. Officer CeCe glanced up. "We should take a break. I have a few leads to follow up on."

Jackie felt Tom's warm hand land on her shoulder and sagged under its weight. "Come on, honey. Why don't we lie down for a minute?"

Before he'd even finished his suggestion, she was shaking her head. "I can't. I have to be here. I have to help in some way."

He knelt in front of her. "You're not going to be able to help Abby or anybody else if you keel over. Please, let's take a quick break." He raised his hands when she opened her mouth to protest. "Ten minutes. That's all I'm asking."

CeCe placed a hand on her knee. "Go on, Jackie. Let us do our jobs. If there are any new developments, I promise you'll be the first person I tell."

Jackie stood, and for the first time since Abby's abduction, noted the activity around her. Her living room, dining room, and the kitchen had all been commandeered and transformed into a makeshift headquarters. Laptops sat on every flat surface available, two unfamiliar men were talking on their phones, and somebody—probably Olivia—had made a fresh pot of coffee.

The Christmas tree they had found such joy in lighting and decorating was shoved as far into the corner as possible and stood at an angle. Nobody had bothered to plug it in.

"Somebody should water the tree," she said.

"All right, honey," Tom agreed.

"I'll do it," Fiona volunteered and moved into the kitchen to get some water. All three of the Harper sisters were present, along with Alex, although they appeared to be at a loss for what to do. Jackie recognized Officer Brad. She and Olivia had gone to high school with him, and he'd been very helpful with Olivia's case last year, but the other people were strangers.

She heard noise coming from outside and moved toward the window. Brushing the curtain aside, she was surprised to find a mob of news crews and a large crowd camped out on the curb in front of her house.

"Damn vultures," Tom growled behind her. "They started to arrive as soon as the Amber Alert was broadcast."

Jackie wasn't sure how to feel about the media outside her house. A part of her was thankful to them for helping her get the word out about her little girl. Hopefully, someone would see the newscast and contact the police about Abby.

Another part of her was afraid that if they truly were vultures, then she—her hopes, her fears, her daughter—was the carcass they were circling.

Was she using them, or were they using her?

"Come on, Jackie," Tom said as he rubbed her shoulders. "Let's step away from the windows."

She let the edge of the curtain drop back into place and shuffled down the hallway to their bedroom.

Grief was heavy.

She'd heard that expression before but never fully understood how literal it was. She felt as if she'd aged a hundred years in the span of a day; even her joints ached.

The bedroom was quiet and dim, like a tomb. Tom led her to the bed and pulled down the covers, then tucked them up over her shoulders after she climbed in. The mattress sank with his weight as he sat by her hip. She faced away from him, still clutching the toy bunny to her chest, and curled into the fetal position.

He gently stroked her hair, letting silence take over the room. The first sob bubbled up from her chest and cracked the surface, and a steady torrent of tears followed. Tom shifted and wrapped his body around her, holding her as the storm of emotions overpowered her.

She couldn't breathe, she couldn't think, she couldn't *be* without her daughter. Her Abby. Her everything. A black, yawning pit sat in her chest where her heart had been.

Had it only been that morning since she'd held her? How could her arms feel so empty?

The rest of her life stretched out before her—a vast, wretched wasteland without her child. She clutched at Tom's forearms where they wrapped around her chest, wailing into the void until she'd exhausted herself. Until she was nothing. Until, finally, sleep took pity on her.

*

Tom had thought he knew grief.

He'd encountered it plenty of times during his service. Young soldiers crying for their families as they bled out, staining the sand around them. Boys who were playing soccer one minute, on the ground writhing in pain with their legs blasted off by an IED the next. Mothers who clutched the bodies of their loved ones to them, keening in despair at their loss.

Too often, innocent children and civilians were the ones who paid the bill of war.

His time overseas had been rife with the injustice that violence wrought. Yet, at some point, he'd been able to distance himself from it and function well enough to do his job. He'd grown a callus over all but the worst instances.

This was different.

Never had he been rendered this utterly helpless.

The hardened soldier within shifted restlessly in his chest. Tom presumed Randy was behind all of this. The timing was too convenient for this to be a coincidence, and he didn't believe in coincidences, anyway. Unfortunately, until they could find proof, he couldn't do anything about his suspicions.

If he had a target to focus his anger on, he could execute a plan of action. His arms tightened convulsively, bringing Jackie closer to him. Even in her sleep, she cried for her daughter, and it broke his heart.

He lay there for as long as he could, haunted by the echoes of Abby's laughter, the way she called him Tom-tom. How her little arms felt hugging his neck.

If the fear and grief were this bad for him, he couldn't imagine what they were like for Jackie. How could any human bear such a burden?

He moved his weight and carefully extracted his arm out from under her, thankful when she remained asleep. The best thing for her was sleep, but he couldn't sit still any longer.

He crept toward the door and slipped out. From where he stood in the hallway, the activity in the living room was muted, but he could see everyone was working diligently.

"How's she doing?" Mason asked, joining him in the hallway.

"About how you would expect." Tom rubbed the bridge of his nose.

Mason placed a hand on his shoulder. "How are you holding up?"

Tom didn't trust his voice enough to answer. Instead, he shook his head. After a moment of struggling, he said, "How can I be of help? I need something to do."

"You got it." Mason led him to the living room table. "I hope you don't mind, Olivia helped me select a couple of current photos for the posters. We could use some help distributing them around town."

Tom gazed at the recent photo of Abby from the holiday pageant. She was dressed up as an elf, beaming at the camera. Had that only been a few nights ago?

"I'd rather not leave Jackie alone."

Olivia stepped up. "I can keep an eye on her."

Tom noted the bruised circles under her eyes. He doubted any of them would get much rest until Abby was safe at home. "I'm sure she'd appreciate that."

"Fiona, Alex, and I could help hang posters," Liz volunteered. "We could split into partners and hit both sides of town. Plus, the faster we get them up, the better."

"Sounds good. We could even get some up in the surrounding areas." Tom took the pile from Mason. "I'm sure I have some staplers and tape around here. Let's find them and get going."

"Before you go, you have to promise me one thing." Mason stepped close, setting his hands on Tom's shoulders. Tom fought the urge to push him off. "Promise me you won't go after Randy if I let you out of my sight."

"Where would you get an idea like that?" Tom asked.

"Tom"—Mason's voice held a note of warning— "don't make me regret this."

He waved a hand in acknowledgment but made no promises.

CHAPTER TWELVE

TOM TOOK ANOTHER handful of posters and hopped out of the truck. Fiona met him at the telephone post. Between the two of them, they'd developed a fast, efficient method for hanging the signs. One held the poster in place while the other stapled the corners. In the span of fifteen minutes, every post within two blocks held a black-and-white photo of Abby.

Looking up and down the street was like a kick to the gut.

Tom caught Fiona discreetly wiping a tear from the corner of her eye. At this point, neither of them felt like talking. Which, if he was being honest, wasn't a big change for him, but she was usually a chatterbox.

He glanced over and found her staring at the Christmas display in a shop window. "How're you holding up, Fiona?"

She shifted her attention to him. "Y'know. Probably better than you or Jackie, but not by much."

They crossed an intersection and saw four other people hanging signs down the next street. It looked like the whole town was out in force.

"We're almost out of posters. What do you say we head over to Brunswick and get some hung up over there?" he said.

"Fine, we can hit the college campus, too. I know where most of the community boards are located, and I'm sure the librarians would be willing to make a few more copies for us." They headed back toward the truck.

"Sounds good." He hesitated. "If you're up for it, I'd like to make another stop while we're there."

She didn't look surprised. "I figured as much." Fiona turned up the heat and rubbed her hands in front of the vent.

"What do you mean?"

"Why do you think Mason paired me up with you? He assumed you'd try to go talk to him. He assumed I'd be a good influence and talk you out of it."

He gripped the steering wheel. "I reckoned it would be best to talk to him without Jackie there. Her presence would only provoke him."

"What? And yours won't?"

Tom's jaw clenched. "Look, you can stay in the truck."

"Hell no. I'm not trying to stop you. The cops have already questioned him, but I still feel we should go see what he has to say about all of this."

"You do?"

"Yes, I do." She rolled her eyes. "Why does everybody regard me as some sort of soft, wishy-washy person?"

He snorted. "Probably because you use terms like *wishy-washy*."

At his dubious look, she said, "Fine, I admit that most of the time it's probably true, but not when it comes to finding Abby. We should be doing everything we can to find her, and that includes asking her biological father what he knows about her disappearance."

Finally! Someone who agreed with him. "I can't tell you how happy I am to hear you say that."

"Good." She leaned over to look at the odometer. "Now that we have that covered, can you step on it? I hope you're not driving like an old man on my account. Jackie said he's staying at that apartment building near I-295."

The truck surged forward. "Yeah, I know where it is. Randy's address was listed on the court summons," he muttered.

By the time they reached the parking lot, they were antsy and wired for trouble. Fiona's knee had been bouncing for the past five minutes. She wiped her damp palms on the front of her jeans. "How do you want to play this?"

The building was cheap and impersonal, standard construction for inexpensive apartments. There were two floors, and every unit had a door facing the parking lot. Its painted white façade had faded to a dingy gray, and the brown trim was chipped in most places. The door with Randy's address was visible through the wrought-iron railing on the veranda upstairs.

"I'm going to walk up to the door and knock," he said, then gave her a heavy look. "It might be better if you stayed in the car."

"Like hell. Besides, how am I going to stop you from pummeling each other from down here?"

"I wasn't planning on hitting him."

Fiona raised an eyebrow. "You may not be planning on it, but if your fist 'accidentally' connects with his nose, there's nothing that can be done about it, right?"

Tom smirked but didn't admit to anything. "Fine, let's go," he grumbled. A moment later, he added, "You're a brat, you know that?"

"Yeah, yeah." Fiona bumped her shoulder against his. "But I'm still right."

Moments later, they were standing in front of a stained door that had seen better days. Tom pounded on it. "Randy! Open up!"

They heard something fall to the floor with a thump. Footsteps paused just inside the door. Half a minute later, it cracked open. "Wha' tha' fuck do ya wan'?" The words were accompanied by a whiff of liquor.

"Nice, asshole. Your daughter's missing, and you decide it's time to go on a bender?" Tom slammed his hand against the door and pushed it open. Randy stumbled back, allowing them access into the room.

"What do you care?" Randy said indignantly. "She's my daughter, not yours!"

"Thank goodness, she takes after her mother." Tom glared at the other man in disgust. He was standing in boxers and a black T-shirt that had a hole in the collar. "For fuck's sake, go put some pants on and wash your face. I have some questions I want to ask you."

"The cops were already here and asked their questions."

"Good for them." He took a step closer. "Pull yourself together, or I will. Don't make me ask you again."

Fear and resentment warred in his expression, but a second later, Randy headed toward the bathroom. "Fine. Don't touch anything."

"I'll go pour him a glass of water. Don't do anything until I get back," Fiona said before exiting the room. On her way to the kitchen, Fiona stopped and spun on her heel. "Tom, I mean it. I may agree with you about questioning him, but I refuse to be an accessory to murder."

"What? I'm relaxed." He slid out one of the two chairs at the tiny dining room table and sat. "See? I can't exactly murder anybody while seated." Strictly speaking, that wasn't true, but it was probably better if she didn't know that.

The sun sat low on the horizon sending long shadows dancing across the room. Tom and Fiona sat at the dining room table facing Randy, who was perched on the edge of a couch cushion. He kept fidgeting and shifting his gaze back and forth between the two of them.

He took another sip of the water Fiona had retrieved for him. "I don't understand why you're here. I've already been grilled by the cops, and there's nothing else to tell."

Randy wasn't exactly sober, but Tom was happy his speech was no longer slurred. It didn't stifle his urge to wring the asshole's neck, though.

Was he wasting his time? Would it be better if he was out there looking for Abby? Better to come right out and ask the question that was on everyone's mind. Tom was sure he'd detect if the other man was lying. If he did, that would point Tom to the next course of action. "Did you have anything to do with Abby's disappearance?"

"What? No!" Randy's outrage appeared genuine, even though the accusation couldn't have surprised him. Surely, the cops had asked him the same question.

"Why should I believe you?"

Randy chewed the hangnail on his middle finger. As though realizing what he was doing, he brought his hand down and took another sip. "I don't know, man. Because I didn't?"

"What were you doing at the time that she was abducted?"

His finger crept back toward his mouth. "I don't have an alibi, if that's what you're asking. I was here, sleeping."

"During the middle of the day?" Tom leaned forward.

Randy put his hands up, as though warding him off. "I swear!" He bent over and started to reach under the couch, but Tom moved to stop him. "Easy, easy... I'm getting a bottle. See?" He brandished the empty bottle of vodka, cheap enough that it was a miracle it hadn't burned straight through his internal organs. "It's been hard to stay on the wagon lately. After the school play, I was feeling sorry for myself and stopped by the store for this. Kept me oblivious for most of the night, and I wound up sleeping it off all the next day."

"And, that whole time, you didn't see anybody?"

"No. I mean, I ordered pizza later that night but nothing during the afternoon." He gestured toward the small black trash can sitting by the TV stand. "You can see the box is still in there. My housekeeper has the year off." The joke fell flat given the circumstances, but not out of character from what Tom had learned about the guy.

Fiona, who had been watching the whole exchange, got up and inspected the box. "Yeah, the box still has the receipt on it, and the time and date corroborate his story."

"That still doesn't prove anything," Tom said. "You probably knew the police would suspect you and could have called it in. Hell, you could have had someone else here to accept the delivery."

Randy started shaking his head before Tom had even finished. "No, man. No! I would never do that to a child." Tears welled in his red-rimmed eyes and began tracking down his cheeks. "All I wanted was to sober up and have a chance to be her daddy. If Jackie really thinks I'm capable of harming my own baby, that sweet little girl…" He hiccupped. "That sweet little girl! How could somebody steal her like that? Every time I think about what they could be doing—" Randy clapped his hand over his mouth, not daring to continue.

"Shit." Tom pounded the back of his head against the wall behind him. It would have been easier if Randy was the bad guy. At least Abby would be relatively safe.

On the other hand, a strange man taking her? The possibilities stemming from that scenario made him shudder. Randy nodded, reached down, and extracted another half-empty bottle then twisted the cap off before taking a healthy swig. "I know, man. I wish I had taken her, too."

Tom took a step back from that mental black hole and changed tactics. "You've been hanging around a lot these last few days. Have you seen anything suspicious?"

"You make me sound like a stalker," Randy grumbled, but at Tom's raised eyebrow, he closed his eyes and mulled over the question. "Not that I can recall. Every time I've seen her, she's been with family."

"Shit." The answer left Tom feeling deflated. To Fiona, he said, "We should get going. Mason is going to wonder where we are."

Her shoulders slumped. "All right."

He contemplated Randy, who was taking another swig from the bottle. "I still think you're an asshole."

Randy's finger shot up. The tip was red from where he'd been chewing on it. "Right back at ya."

Tom ignored the gesture. "But if you want any hope of

convincing Jackie that you're ready to visit Abby, you gotta stop drinking that shit."

Randy lowered the bottle and peered into its depths with blood-shot eyes. "You're right." The confession was barely above a whisper, but Tom recognized what admitting it had cost him.

Tom extended his hand toward him. "Give me the bottle and let me get it out of here. If your parole officer finds out you've been drinking—"

"—then I can kiss any hope of seeing my daughter again good-bye, assuming we find her."

Tom's face flashed with determination. "We'll find her."

"Do you have any more, Randy?" The kindness and concern in Fiona's voice were more than Tom had been able to manage.

With a resigned sigh, he reached down to grab a bottle that had been shoved under the couch. "No, but can you take this empty bottle with you, too? Might as well get rid of all the evidence I can." He ran fingers through his greasy, thinning hair. "Of course, if she decides to give me a blood test, I'm screwed."

"Then lay low until it's out of your system. Sleep it off," Tom suggested.

"Right."

As they stepped from the sad apartment, Randy leaned against the doorjamb with the door slightly cracked. They were halfway down the stairs before he said, "Y'know, I was kind of surprised to see Jackie had made up with her parents, especially given the way things ended."

"What?" Tom stopped and turned to face Randy. "She hasn't made up with them. It's been years since they've talked, let alone seen each other."

"Huh, I could have sworn that was Jackie's father I saw speaking to Abby in the tree lot." His posture curled self-consciously. "I mean, it's been six years. What the hell do I know?"

"You'd know a lot more if you sobered up," Tom said, but his words lacked the bite they would've had earlier.

Randy looked down at his empty hands. They'd already started to shake. "Maybe I should."

CHAPTER THIRTEEN

"ABBY." JACKIE WOKE in the dark and immediately felt her daughter's absence. What must she be experiencing? Fresh tears welled as guilt crushed her. "I'm a terrible mother."

"Oh, Jackie." Olivia sighed. "No, you're not. You're a wonderful mother."

She hadn't realized someone else was in the room but didn't bother to acknowledge her friend's words. "What time is it?"

"A little after five." She paused. "I was hoping you'd sleep a bit longer."

"How could I sleep at all?" Jackie sat up and folded her knees to her chest. "I've failed my daughter."

"No, you haven't. Don't say that." Olivia rose from the chair she'd been sitting on in the corner to wrap her arms around her friend.

"I've lost her! In what world does that make me a good mother?" Jackie choked on her grief. "Have there been any new leads?" She knew the answer before she'd even asked. If there were, Olivia would have woken her up.

And yet, her heart still plummeted when her friend shook her head.

"That's bad, right?" She dropped her head to her knees and tugged on her hair, willing her brain to recall any details from the afternoon that might help. "I remember hearing that most kidnappers who are looking for a ransom contact the parents in the first few hours. What does it mean that nobody has called asking for money?"

Olivia tightened her grip as if trying to force strength into Jackie. "It's too early to be jumping to conclusions. Mason, Brad, and countless others are doing everything they can to make sure Abby comes home safely."

"And I'm lying in bed."

"Jackie—"

Raising a hand, she squeezed her eyes shut and counted to ten. With a deep breath, Jackie gave her friend a look. "I want to get up."

"Okay." Olivia stood. "I'll go talk to Mason. Maybe we can do something to help in the search."

"Thank you."

Olivia slipped out of the bedroom, shutting the door behind her. It was the first time Jackie had been left alone since Abby's disappearance, and the silence of the room was unnerving.

The security tape kept scratching at her memory, but she couldn't put her finger on what she was missing. She mentally flipped through the images from the monitor and compared them to her own perspective of what happened directly after Abby went missing. The confusion and fear she'd experienced while frantically looking for her child clouded her mind. Jackie struggled to separate her emotions from the actual events and walk back through everything she'd done while looking for Abby.

She'd been checking the racks, had gotten down on her knees....

And the woman from earlier had asked her what she was doing. She'd pointed toward another section of the store and mentioned seeing Abby head in that direction. The video recording had shown her daughter and the lady talking, which confirmed her accounting of events.

Her eyes popped open. The woman had pointed her in the wrong direction! The surveillance had proven she and Abby had talked, but the woman had pointed Jackie in the direction opposite of the one Abby had taken. Had she been an accessory to the abduction?

"Holy shit!" Jackie bounded from the bed and rushed down the hallway. The living room was organized chaos, the noise jarring after the quiet of her room. "Mason, I realized something."

He strode toward her. "Jackie, what is it?"

She explained how the woman she'd seen talking to her daughter in the video had misdirected her during her search. Mason listened. "Are you sure she wasn't simply confused?"

Jackie shook her head. "No, the more I go over it, the more I'm convinced it was intentional. And there's another thing that bothers me about her. She was a little off. The first time Abby and I ran into her, she made me uncomfortable."

"Uncomfortable how?"

"I don't know." Jackie tossed up her hands and struggled to put her feeling into words. "Abby had been playing hide-and-seek and nearly ran into her. I'd cautioned her to be more careful, and in response, the woman quoted the Bible at us."

"It's not that uncommon to quote the Bible," Mason hedged. "Are you sure you're not reading too much into the encounter?"

"It's not the fact that she referred to a Bible passage. It's the fact that she referenced a fairly strict interpretation and quoted it verbatim." Jackie shrugged when Mason raised an eyebrow. "I may not be religious anymore, but much of my childhood was spent learning scripture well enough to recognize even the most obscure passages."

"What did she quote?"

"The first time she said, 'He that spareth his rod hateth his son: but he that loveth him chasteneth him betimes', which I took to mean she felt I was being too lenient with my daughter. At the time, I remember thinking it sounded a bit harsh. It also felt intrusive for a stranger to be commenting on my parenting style, not to mention judgmental and rude. Then again, Abby almost bowled her over. I decided to give her comment a pass and not say anything.

"You've seen it. Nowadays, everybody has an opinion about how you should raise your child." She gestured dismissively. "I tried to blow it off and move on."

"You said, 'the first time'. Was there another instance where she quoted the Bible to you?"

"Yes, there was." Jackie's brow wrinkled as she recalled. "It was after Abby had disappeared. She said, 'But Jesus said, Suffer little children, and forbid them not, to come unto me: for of such is the kingdom of heaven'."

At Mason's obvious confusion, she went on to explain, "It's a reference to a passage from the book of Mark. I never considered it to be sinister until I heard her say it while I was searching for Abby. At the time, I wanted to say, 'No, my daughter is too young to go to God.'"

"Let me make sure I understand you. What you're saying is that there was a woman quoting Bible verses to you who pointed you in the wrong direction when you were looking for your daughter."

She chewed her lip, doubt creeping in. "Am I grasping at straws?"

"On the contrary, this is definitely something we should be following up on. You already had a chance to watch the video. Is there a good image of her face on the recording?"

"Yes, there is."

"Thank you, Jackie. This could be helpful."

"I wish it had come to me earlier."

"Don't beat yourself up. The brain works differently during traumatic situations. Memories and connections aren't always obvious. Patterns can be hard to discern."

"But... I was sleeping this whole time!"

"Which could be the very reason why you managed to piece it together." He leaned down to be eye level with her. "Don't do this to yourself, Jackie. Nothing good will come from second-guessing everything."

She had a lump of unshed tears stuck in her throat. "I know you're right," she rasped.

"We've already compiled a list of the people in the video and are working on identifying them and contacting them for questioning. However, I'll be sure to have them prioritize this woman. We can get an image and description of her to the media as a person of interest, as well. Are you going to be okay?"

"Yes. Is there anything I can do to help?" He hesitated. "I'm going to go crazy if I don't stay busy," she pleaded.

Olivia stepped in. "Jackie, could you help me put together a meal for these guys? They haven't eaten since they got the call, and people are going to require fuel to keep going."

"I can do that." She looked around before following Olivia into the kitchen. "I thought Tom was out here, but I haven't seen him. Where did he go?"

"He's with Fiona, Alex, and Liz hanging missing-person posters around town."

She pressed her palms against the countertop and bowed her head, trying to catch her breath as another stab of pain pierced her chest.

"Hey, how are you holding up?" Olivia rubbed a hand across her back. "You realize that you don't have to do this. I can put dinner together by myself."

She shook her head before straightening. "No, I'll go mad if I sit around and do nothing. It's better if I stay busy and feel like I'm helping."

Her friend gave her a hug. "Makes sense. In that case, let's see what you have in the fridge and feed these people."

Minutes later, Jackie found herself cutting carrots for a salad while the smell of onions and garlic filled the air. Ordinarily, it would have been comforting, but the banality of the moment and the dire circumstances was uncomfortably absurd.

She inhaled sharply as the edge of the knife sliced into her finger. "Shit."

"Are you okay?"

Tears streamed down her cheeks as she sucked on the injured digit. "No!" The knife clattered as she flung it into the sink. Crimson drops of blood were strewn across the cutting board. "I am not okay!"

Firm hands drew her into a hard, familiar chest. "Come here." Tom's voice was deep and reassuring.

After a moment, she mumbled into his shirt. "Weren't you hanging up posters?"

"I was, but I wanted to get back before you woke up. Fiona, Liz, and Alex have taken over, along with the rest of the town."

"What do you mean?"

He traced a thumb along her jawline. "You didn't think everybody would sit around after seeing that Amber Alert, did you? The whole town is out looking, hanging up posters, walking the woods, you name it. Whatever they can do to help."

Fresh tears tracked down her cheeks. "I should be out there with them."

"No." He drew her closer. "You should be right here in case the kidnappers try to contact you or if there are any new developments. Speaking of which, I may have learned some news." At those words, Jackie's head shot up. "But I don't want you to get your hopes up until we find out more," Tom cautioned.

Fear and hope warred inside her. "Tell me."

"I will, but only if you let me take a look at that cut." After inspecting it for a moment, he said, "Good. It doesn't look too deep. Let's get it cleaned and wrapped up. We'll talk while I do that. Olivia, you got this?"

She was already washing the cutting board and knife. "Of course, don't worry about me. Dinner will be ready in about thirty minutes."

"Thank you." Tom held Jackie's other hand and took her to the bathroom, then sat her down on the toilet.

After collecting the necessary items from the medicine cabinet, he knelt in front of her. "Mason told me you remembered something."

"It may not mean anything." She shrugged. "She's probably a crazy old lady. I still suspect Randy is behind this."

"I'm not entirely sure about that. Fiona and I went and had a little talk with him."

"*What?*" She moved to pull her hand away, but Tom held it firmly in his.

"This might sting a little." Carefully, he cleaned the cut with some hydrogen peroxide before softly blowing on it. "Let me tell you, Mason was none too pleased when he heard what we'd done. Thankfully, Fiona talked him down."

"Was he of any help?"

"Overall, no. It looked like he'd been hitting the bottle pretty hard this last week. I'd hate to be his parole officer. However, right before we left, he did say something that was confusing."

She rolled her eyes. "Randy is always confusing. Or drunk. Toward the end there, it was both. What did he say?"

Tom wrapped a bandage around the pad of her finger. "When was the last time you talked with your parents?"

"M-My parents?" The change in subject had her wrinkling her brow in confusion. She looked at the ceiling and blew out a breath while she tried to remember.

After a moment of contemplation, she returned her attention to him. "About six years ago, I'd guess? It was after I told them I was pregnant but before Abby was born." She glanced toward the door. "They aren't here, are they?"

"No, no," he assured her. "Nothing like that. After talking to Randy, I'm confident he's not our guy. However, when I asked him if he'd noticed anything suspicious while he'd been trailing Abby, he mentioned seeing your parents. Specifically, your dad."

"That's not possible." A tingle of memory touched the corner of her mind but flitted away before she could fully realize it. "I can't believe how long it's been since I've seen or spoken to either one of my parents." She rubbed at the headache pounding in her temple.

"How terrible is that?" Jackie waved away whatever answer he was about the give. "Never mind. Was Randy sure?"

"He appeared to be certain."

"Do you think he was trying to redirect attention off himself? He's gotta realize that he's a suspect."

"That wasn't the impression I got." Tom hedged, "Speaking of which, I checked in with CeCe when I arrived. She said they obtained a warrant to search his vehicle and didn't come up with anything."

"Is that good news or bad news?" At this point, it was hard telling what was up or down.

"I'm not sure. It is what it is."

A knock on the door interrupted anything else he might have said. Mason poked his head into the room. "Sorry to intrude."

"What's going on?" Jackie's voice was tight with anticipation.

"We got a hit on that woman you told us about. Apparently, she's got priors for harassment and disrupting the peace. She belongs to a fringe religious group. Y'know, the kind who likes to wave signs and shout at the funerals of people they consider to be sinners? She and a few others got out of hand a couple of months back and wound up sitting in a jail cell for a few days."

"A fringe religious group? You mean like a cult?" she asked.

"Some would probably classify them as that. If not a full-fledged cult, then close. Have you ever heard of His Glory's Children?"

"That's the same Christian fundamentalist group my parents joined back when I was in high school."

"What the hell would they have to do with Abby?" Tom asked.

Mason stuffed his hands in his pockets and leaned back on the doorjamb. "Maybe nothing. We won't know until we ask her. Gonna bring her in for questioning as a potential witness and see what shakes out. Anyway, I figured you'd like to know." He moved to leave.

"Mason?" Jackie asked.

"Yeah?"

"Are you looking into my parents?"

"We're looking into all leads." Despite his concerned tone, the eyes that met hers were cool and focused—what Olivia referred to as his 'cop eyes'.

"I understand," Jackie said. "Will you please tell me what you find out?"

"Will do," he confirmed.

Tom put everything away and washed his hands. He looked down at Jackie still seated on the toilet. She was inspecting his handiwork, but her mind was somewhere else. "Are you okay?"

Her shoulders tensed before dropping. "I wish people would stop asking me that. No, I am not okay"—she stood and faced him— "but I'm managing. Until we find Abby, that's all I can do."

"That's fair." He held her hands in his. "Nobody expects you to be fine. We're simply checking in with you to see how you're holding up. A lot of people love you." He pressed his forehead to hers. "I love you."

A single tear trailed down her cheek. "I love you, too."

"And we will find her, Jackie. I won't stop until we do."

"I'm counting on it," she whispered.

CHAPTER FOURTEEN

ONE OF THE tech people—Jackie couldn't remember all of their names—looked up from his screen as she and Tom entered the living room. "These guys are some real nutjobs, boss."

"That's what I'm discovering over here, too. Let me see what you've got." Mason raised his head as Tom and Jackie joined the group. His look made Jackie feel like he'd weighed and assessed her state of well-being in one glance. "Jackie, could you go check in with Olivia? I heard a crash in there, and she might need some help."

As far as excuses went, it was pretty thin. They both knew that Olivia regularly ran a kitchen three times larger and fed at least four times as many people, but Jackie took the hint. "Sure, Mason."

"Thanks," he said before gesturing toward Tom.

Tom gave her a kiss on the temple before walking to the officer on the couch and peering over his shoulder.

Jackie's lips were a rueful twist as she contemplated their actions. A part of her wanted to assert her right to be informed about what was going on, but another side of her trusted that they were excluding her for a reason. She wasn't sure she wanted to open that can of worms. Deciding to let it go, she moved into the kitchen. "Hi, Olivia. Sorry for my outburst."

Olivia was grating parmesan cheese into a bowl but set it down to give her a hug. "I'm surprised it didn't happen earlier. It's impressive you're even standing upright."

"No promises it's going to stay like that." Jackie felt exhausted, despite her nap. "Anything I can do to help?"

Jackie took stock of everything on the counter. All the dirty dishes had been washed and put away. A buffet was set up, starting with utensils, paper plates, and napkins, then followed by a salad and separate bowls for dressings, pasta, and sauce. At the end of the line, there were loaves of garlic bread cut up and ready to be torn into.

"It looks amazing, Olivia. How did you manage to find all of this stuff in my kitchen?"

"Liz and Alex stopped by the grocery store before heading out again. I'm happy I could do something to help, even if it's simply feeding everybody."

"Keeping people fed is a lot." Jackie paused. "Mason was intent on getting me out of the room. Have you heard anything?"

Her friend gave her a cautious look. "I heard Randy's car was clean."

"That's what Tom said."

"And, did he mention there may be a connection to your parents?"

"Yes." Jackie leaned forward. "How can that be possible? Randy mentioned seeing Abby talking to my dad, but I haven't seen either of my parents since before she was born. How would they even recognize her? You remember how extreme they got toward the end there."

If anyone understood why she had cut off all contact with them, Olivia would. "Trust me, I remember, Jackie. When we were growing up, I never would have guessed they'd abandon their pregnant daughter. My impression was you had a close, loving relationship. Granted, they were strict, but still!"

"You're telling me. They got weird and much more fanatical after they switched churches. My last two years of high school were hell."

"That still doesn't explain why they would show up, after all these years, and take your daughter away. It doesn't make sense."

"I thought the same thing, but..." Jackie rubbed her temple. "Could it really be a coincidence that there was a lady quoting sinister Bible verses at me the same day my daughter went missing? And that she belongs to the same group my parents joined all those years ago?"

"Are you saying they're related?"

"I think it's likely. At this point, it's kind of a stretch that it wouldn't be, right?"

"That's what we were considering as well," Mason said from the doorway. "Everything we've been reading about His Glory's Children—HGC—indicates they've become more extreme these past few years. On top of that, but given their name, it's not too much to assume they prioritize children."

"Probably want to indoctrinate them young," Jackie muttered. "I got into a lot of fights with my parents my junior and senior years. I remember during one particularly bad argument, they said I was destined to be a sinner because they hadn't 'gotten to me' in time."

Olivia threaded an arm around her waist. "I'm glad you weren't brainwashed by those crazy people."

She leaned her head on her friend's shoulder. "Thanks, me too. Don't get me wrong, I still have faith in some type of God, but religion and I have a rocky relationship."

CeCe walked into the kitchen during that last comment and fingered the cross around her neck. "Jackie, so you know, my whole church and I have been praying for your daughter all day. I figure it doesn't hurt and could do some good."

"Thanks, CeCe. That means a lot." Jackie moved toward the door. "Everyone, help yourselves to the food. I'm going to let the others know to take a break."

CHAPTER FIFTEEN

TOM GAVE JACKIE'S arm a squeeze as she walked past. She'd told him a few things about how she'd been raised, but he had no idea her home life had gotten that bad. Mason had informed him that he was checking to see if there were still ties between her parents and HGC.

Judging by what they knew, he'd be surprised if there weren't a connection. "Jackie, do you have any photos of you and your parents?"

"Somewhere… All my old albums are packed in a box in the basement."

"Great. I think I'll go take a look for them," he said.

"Give me a minute to call in the troops and I'll join you."

He headed down to the basement as she poked her head into the living room. All three techs and the FBI liaison were staring at their monitors and tapping on their devices.

Jackie sidled up to the nearest tech agent, a man named Jesse, and noticed the screen was filled with information about HGC, including the address and a photo of the leader. She hadn't realized they were located so close to town. "Hey, everyone. Dinner is ready."

"Yes! I'm starving." Jesse had the metabolism of a high schooler and looked too young to be working for the FBI. Despite his youthful appearance, he had seemed highly competent when she'd seen him furiously typing at the keyboard earlier.

His coworker pushed her glasses up and gaped at him. "Are you kidding me? You've been snacking on something the whole time we've been here! How can you still be hungry?" she teased. Agent Soo Chen was utterly stunning, but in a muted way, as though she'd made the conscious decision to tone down her looks so they wouldn't be distracting. She wore a basic outfit of black slacks and a white button-down shirt. Jackie had the impression it was a self-imposed uniform that she wore every day—clean, professional, and efficient.

"Whatever, Z. Not all of us can eat like a bird." He stood. "Besides, I work better when I'm fed."

The two of them reminded her of siblings, even though they looked nothing alike. Jesse was a tall, skinny black kid with a short afro, and Soo was barely over five feet tall. She had long, silky black hair that she kept in a simple braid and played with when she was deep in thought. Yet, despite appearances, it was obvious the two of them were family in all the ways that mattered.

Jackie approached the other gentleman, who was tapping intently on his keyboard. Although she'd been distressed when they'd arrived, she'd noticed that this agent was impeccably dressed, from his tie to his cufflinks. His pants were sharply creased down the front of each leg, even after hours of sitting at the computer.

He minimized what was on his screen as she drew near. "What have you guys been working on?" she asked. Jackie wasn't a complete rube when it came to technology—she and her smartphone enjoyed a good working relationship—but her skillset was nothing compared to what she'd glimpsed them doing that afternoon.

"Ma'am, sorry, but most of the information we find is confidential." Special Agent Roger Mann grimaced. He may have been older than the other two, but he looked like he was no more than thirtysomething. Maybe young forties. "To be honest, ma'am, you don't want to know. Trust me when I tell you we're doing everything we can to find your daughter."

"That's exactly what Special Agent in Charge Reyes told Tom when he asked." She looked over at the sharply dressed woman talking on the phone. "You FBI agents are tight-lipped." She faced Roger, startled to find him staring at her. His brown eyes were apologetic. "But if it helps you find my daughter, I promise not to hold it against you."

"I wish I could say more, but when you're in our line of work, there are some things you can't unsee. I'd rather spare you the details, if possible."

She digested that tidbit and was determined not to imagine her daughter in that context. "What about the other two agents? I mean, Jesse strikes me as too young to be subjected to the kind of research you're referring to. Can he even legally buy a drink?"

The question had the desired effect, and she was rewarded with a small smile. "Barely. Hard to believe, right?"

"How does one get into this line of work?" she asked, curious about the team that had taken over her living room.

His warmth vanished and a wistful, distant expression crossed his face. "Sometimes, you don't get to choose. It chooses you." He locked his computer and stood. "If you'll excuse me, I'm gonna get some dinner before Jesse eats it all."

"Of course." She noticed that Agent Marta Reyes was still talking on the phone, and the conversation had gotten progressively more animated. Whatever she was discussing would hopefully help bring Abby home.

As that hope crossed her mind, the fifty-something woman hung up. She stared down at the phone in her hand, her lip curling with disgust.

"Is something wrong?" Jackie asked.

Her head flew up, and determination had her pressing her lips. "Wrong? No. Difficult?" She sighed and rubbed a temple with her left hand. "Maybe."

"What's going on?" Jackie moved to stand by her. "Agent Reyes, please. The not knowing is almost as bad as everything else."

"Marta. You can call me Marta." Compassion flooded her warm, brown eyes. She placed her hands on her hips. "Trust me when I tell you that not knowing is sometimes not as bad as knowing, but I promise you that I will not give up."

Fear shivered down her spine, but Jackie swallowed it down. "What can you tell me?"

"That the stupid idiot I was talking to clearly hasn't met someone like me before," she answered with ferocity. As though remembering where she was, she took a deep breath, and with its exhalation, her mask of professionalism fell back into place.

Jackie decided she preferred the former fiery version of Marta. Getting a glimpse of that passion lying beneath the surface was oddly reassuring. "Why are they giving you a hard time?"

"Because everybody is afraid of this turning into another Waco, which means getting a judge to sign off on a search warrant is proving difficult. They want more details and more proof, in order to cover their bureaucratic asses. Now, stop interrogating me and let me do my job."

She squeezed Jackie's hand to soften the blow of her brusque words then began dialing another number. Moments later, the phone was back up to her ear and she'd returned to her corner.

Feeling comforted that Agent Reyes—Marta—would not quit, Jackie vowed to do the same. With that reaffirmation firmly in mind, it was time for her to do her part. She headed down to the basement to join Tom.

She found him on the floor next to an open box labeled *Photo Albums and Scrapbooking*. A photo album lay open in his lap, turned to a page of group pictures from summer camp. He fingered the edge of a picture of her roasting a marshmallow. It had been taken from across a campfire, and sparks were drifting up into the night sky. Jackie's face was cast in flickering light that reflected in her eyes. It was one of her favorites.

"Hey, did you find what you were looking for?"

"Not yet," he answered. "How old were you here?"

"About thirteen or fourteen? It was up at a church camp and was one of the last summers before things started to get bad at home."

"Even then, you were beautiful." He flipped the page. "Why did your parents change so drastically in those last few years?"

"Honestly, I'm not sure. My mom's younger sister, my aunt, passed away during that time, but I can't attribute their extreme transformation to that. I can tell you that they've always been deeply religious, and I was raised on a steady diet of Bible studies and Sunday mornings at church. It's a little surprising that they let me develop such a close relationship with Olivia and her family, considering they weren't a part of our church community."

Tom listened but kept flipping pages. "Why did they?"

"Mainly because John and Lillian Harper were well-liked and respected in this town. They were constantly doing volunteer work in the community. Dad used to tell me this story about how John once helped fix his car. It was right before I was born and money was tight. He couldn't afford a new car, and he couldn't afford to get the one he had repaired, but John made sure his beater of a car was running and that he would be able to get my mom to the hospital when it was time to deliver me."

"From everything I've heard, they were remarkable people."

Jackie smiled at the warm memories. "They were. I felt welcome and a part of the family when I visited them. Lillian treated me like one of her daughters. It meant a lot to me, especially in those last few years of high school when my home life had deteriorated. My heart broke right alongside Olivia's the day they died."

"I can imagine." Tom paused on the last page of the album. "Ah, your graduation pictures. Is this the most recent photo you have of your parents?"

Jackie craned her neck to see the picture in question. "I guess it is." The three of them were standing next to each other but not with each other. Even though her parents were on either side of her, there was a distance between them. None of them touched. She traced a finger across the page, lost in the memory of that day.

Tom put a hand on her knee. "You look miserable."

"I've never been good at hiding my feelings." Jackie tried to keep her tone light but knew he could see how much the distance between her and her parents bothered her.

"May I?" With her permission, he carefully removed the photo from under the protective cover.

"What are you going to do with it?"

"It may be older, but I'm hoping it will help them identify your parents. It could prove whether they were on the premises when Abby was taken."

"Can they do that?" she asked, impressed.

"I'm pretty sure technology is advanced enough that we can use this photo to help ascertain whether your dad appears on the video. Their age won't matter because the computer relies on bone structure in order to find a match.

"Facial recognition. I have to admit that sounds like an episode on one of those crime shows. I never imagined we'd have to use it on my family."

"Look on the bright side"—he stood before helping her up— "it could also eliminate them as suspects."

"True." She bit her lip. "Which possibility is worse? That my parents could be involved, or that it's a complete stranger? Either way, I want my daughter back."

"Let's head upstairs and get this to them. Hopefully, it's a fast process and we can get some answers." He clasped her to him and kissed the crown of her head. Despite the warmth of his body, her arms ached with emptiness. "Then, I want you to promise me that you'll eat something."

"I'm not hungry," she mumbled into the front of his shirt.

"Then eat because it will keep your energy up for your daughter's sake."

She leaned away. "That's a low blow."

"I'm sorry." He gave her another soft kiss, this time on her lips. "It also happens to be true. You have to take care of yourself. Please, let me help you."

When she acquiesced, he gave her an approving look then led her back upstairs.

CHAPTER SIXTEEN

TOM REGISTERED THE minute Jackie realized her father was involved. He'd been standing next to her as they all crowded in a semicircle around the computer monitor after the program pinged the notification that it had a match. She'd been determined to have a front-row seat, and the fire in her face had warned Mason not to bother asking her to leave the room.

He'd felt her whole body stiffen as her right hand came up to cover her mouth. When he'd tried to put his arm around her shoulders, she'd brushed him aside and rushed to the bathroom.

Everybody shifted their weight uncomfortably and refused to look at each other as they heard her retching. Moments after she'd exited the bathroom and hadn't returned, Tom excused himself to stand helplessly outside their bedroom door.

"Honey? Jackie? Can I come in?" The silence from behind the door was even more disconcerting than the sounds of her getting sick.

"Please, Jackie. We're in this together. Don't shut me out." Tom rested his brow against the door frame, pondering his next move. He wanted to respect her privacy, but he also wanted to comfort her. Deciding her comfort took priority, he cracked the door and peered into the dim room. "Jackie?"

When there was no answer, he stepped over the threshold. A

sweater hung from an open drawer, and the closet doors were wide open as though someone had rummaged through her clothes in a rush.

The room was empty.

Tom's stomach dropped, and he rushed to the sliding glass doors that led to a postage-stamp-sized patio in the backyard. He heard an engine start in the driveway. "Shit."

Sprinting through the backyard, he arrived in time to see her car's headlights heading down the street. "Son of a bitch! What the hell are you doing, Jackie?"

He dashed back into the bedroom and headed straight for his coat in the closet by the front door.

"Where are you going, Tom?" Mason asked.

"Jackie's not feeling well. I'm going to the store for her."

The worry lines across his friend's forehead deepened, and Tom felt bad for lying to him. However, until he knew what Jackie had planned, he wasn't about to rat her out to anybody, even if that someone was a good friend. Besides, if he didn't tell Mason what was going on, his friend would be able to honestly say he didn't know when asked about it later.

"Damn. I'm sorry, man. It's been a long, rough day for her."

Tom paused while putting his coat on. "It has been for all of us. You're affected by this as much as we are."

Mason's head hung for a moment before he gathered himself. "Do you want me to tell Olivia to sit with her while you're gone?"

He shook his head. "No. She wants to be left alone for a little while. I won't be long."

"I understand. We'll be here if she wants us."

"Thanks, man."

Tom strode out the door and climbed into his truck. He had a pretty good idea where she was headed. For the first time in a long time, he wished he'd kept his military rifle. That idea scared him almost as much as everything else that had happened that day.

In fact, the only thing that would cause him to revert back to the violence of his past was if either Jackie or Abby ended up hurt. With that potential outcome in mind, he slammed his foot on the gas, determined to catch Jackie before she got to His Glory's Children's compound.

*

Jackie sat at the end of the gated driveway and contemplated her next move. Leaving the house had been fueled by pure instinct, but that had evaporated once she'd arrived.

She slammed her hands on the steering wheel and reminded herself that this wasn't the time to doubt herself. Her daughter's life was at stake. Since she was here, she was determined to search every inch of this house until she got her daughter back. Her parents and everybody else would have to get the fuck out of her way.

Fired up, she was about to exit the car when there was a tap on the window. In any other circumstance, she would have been embarrassed by the way she jumped and yelped in surprise.

Her heart beat erratically as she rolled down her window. "Yes?"

The fifty-something man with salt-and-pepper hair scowled down at her. He held a hunting rifle in his hand, and his face was a foreboding thundercloud. What did it say about her that she wasn't sure which one was more intimidating, the gun or his expression?

"May I help you?" he asked in a deep voice that rumbled like an imminent storm.

"Um, yes. I'm here to see my parents."

"Who are your parents?"

"Mark and Mary Davis."

His lips pursed as he gave her a once over. "I've never seen you here before."

Jackie hesitated before admitting, "We've been estranged for many years."

He narrowed his eyes. "Why are you coming to visit them now?"

"Because I have some news that they may want to hear. It's regarding their granddaughter."

When she mentioned Abby, his stance grew even more defensive. His feet spread farther apart, and he shifted his rifle into both hands. Apparently, he was familiar with the news reports. "Give me the message, and I'll make sure they get it."

Her jaw clenched, but it wouldn't help if she lost her patience with him. "I'm sorry, but that won't do. It's of a personal nature, and I guarantee they won't want anybody outside of the family to know."

"There are no secrets from God, for we are all His children," he intoned. It was a bit jarring hearing it come from a dude who looked like a biker with on his knuckles and plastered across the front of his neck, but Jackie didn't doubt he meant every word.

"All the same, sir, once I discuss the matter with them, they can choose whether or not they feel like sharing it with the rest of the... children." She stumbled over the word, unable to hide the skepticism in her voice.

"Give me a minute." Her would-be guard stepped away from the door and drew a slim phone from his pocket. Jackie was glad to see the cult didn't have an aversion to technology, at least.

Moments later, he came back to the car.

"You've been granted permission to enter the Kingdom. However, no vehicles are allowed at the big house. You'll have to park your vehicle in the parking lot by the guard gate and leave your keys with him."

"Wait, what? You guys want to take my keys?" Her stomach sank. How was she going to be able to get her daughter out of there without her car?

He crossed his arms. "No, what I want to do is deny you access altogether, but unfortunately, I've been overruled. You're going to have to follow the same regulations everybody else does if you want to visit your parents."

Knowing it was a losing battle, she bit back the retort on the tip of her tongue but couldn't help rolling her eyes. "Fine."

"Pull through the gate and give your name and keys to the guard there. His name is Kenny." He leaned into the opened window and pushed his face close enough that she could smell the coffee on his breath. "I'm warning you. I will be watching. Don't try any funny business. If you deviate from my instructions in any way, we will press trespassing charges against you. Do you understand?"

She swallowed. "Yes."

He smirked. "Good girl."

She chafed at the term, hating how infantilizing it sounded. She was a full-grown woman, not some little girl who should be chastised. Shaking her head, she put the car into gear and reminded herself that she had bigger fish to fry. Her fingers tapped an impatient rhythm on the steering wheel while she waited for the old gate to creak open.

Once there was a wide enough gap, she moved forward. A guard shack sat directly on the other side of the gate, in the middle of a pool of fluorescent light from the streetlamp above.

She parked in the middle of three spots, noting that her car was the only vehicle in the lot.

Determined to see this through, no matter what, she grabbed her bag and climbed out of the seat. "Oh!" she gasped as the guard stepped forward, cornering her between the open door and the car. He stood uncomfortably close and gave her a leering grin when she tried to sidle away.

"You're Mark and Mary's daughter?" he asked.

"I am, yes." She shifted to the side, not daring to break eye contact.

"I'm going to keep your keys, and I'll have to search your bag before you can go farther."

Jackie instinctively clutched her purse to her chest. "You have to search my bag, too?"

He shrugged without remorse. "Sorry, ma'am, those are the rules."

She reluctantly handed it over.

He hefted the purse, measuring the weight. "What on earth do you have in here, woman?" Before she could answer, he dumped the contents onto the hood of her car.

"Hey!" she protested, but her irritation didn't faze him. She stood agape as he examined her phone, gray wallet; sunglasses case; a pair of cheap black stretchy gloves; the pack of tissues and wet wipes that stayed in her bag because Abby always had a runny nose or mess to clean up; emergency packs of fruit snacks and peanut butter crackers; lip balm because her lips grew chapped in the winter; a small pack of crayons; a pad of paper filled with drawings of happy-faced stick people, flowers, suns, and rainbows; a rock Abby had insisted on keeping because it sparkled in the sun, which somehow never made it out of her bag; and a couple of tampons because—well, you never knew when you might need them. He pawed through all of it with absolutely no regard.

Satisfied that nothing could be used as a weapon, he stepped back and gestured toward the pile. Stalking forward, she began placing everything back into her handbag, including the rock.

"I'm keeping your phone." He sounded like he was remarking on the time of day.

Jackie's heart sank further. "What? No. You can't do that." No car, no phone... and no one knew she'd come here. Once she entered the house, she would truly be on her own.

"I can if you want to continue." He slowed his words as though he considered her dimwitted. "Our residents are very private. We wouldn't want you taking photos of anything you might see and have them wind up on the internet."

"I'd never do that," she protested but knew it was useless. Both of the guards had been implacable. "Fine," she grumbled.

His smug, patronizing sneer when she handed the phone over grated on her nerves, but she held her tongue. "Then you're all set. The house is that way. Stick to the driveway and don't wander off into the woods." He leaned forward. "Trust me, we'll know," he warned in an exaggerated whisper.

She dug the gloves out of her bag then zipped it up and slung it on her shoulder. The weight felt familiar and comforting. Without the benefit of the streetlight, the way ahead appeared ominous. "How far is it from here?"

"'Bout a quarter of a mile. You'll see it."

Jackie took a fortifying breath and proceeded down the driveway. The ground was carpeted with pine needles and rotting leaves layered over gravel. Snow lingered in the shadows along the edges, and she could hear unseen creatures rustling among the shrubs. At least it hadn't snowed in the last week and most of the ground cover had a chance to melt from the last storm.

Still, the sharp bite to the air had her wrapping her sweater a little tighter around her body. She should have given this plan a little more thought before rushing over here half-cocked and ill-prepared. At least she could have brought a coat!

It was wishful thinking. There was no way she would have been able to sneak out past the group of FBI agents in the living room. A pang of guilt stabbed her in the heart. Jackie knew they were doing everything they could for her daughter, but there was no way she could wait another minute without at least trying to do something.

A part of her hoped a thread of familial connection still existed between her and her parents and that she'd be able to reach them somehow. Jackie remembered the time directly after they'd abandoned her. Their betrayal had preceded Randy leaving her, and she'd been devastated. Somedays, she had felt as though every fiber of her body had been filled with pain. The only things that had gotten her through that difficult time had been the life growing inside her and her friendship with Olivia.

It wasn't until after she'd given birth and was holding her daughter in her arms for the first time that her pain had been tempered with confusion. Staring down at her daughter's sweet face, holding her precious hand in hers, Jackie knew she'd never be able to abandon her child. No matter what Abby did, she had vowed then and there to be there for her.

The anger and fear she'd felt when she'd first realized her father was the man from the video twisted in her gut. Why had he taken her daughter? How could her parents—for if her father was involved, her mother surely was, too—have done something this terrible? Did they hate her that much?

She angrily dashed the tears that fell down her cheeks, refusing to give in to the despair that sat heavy in her heart. The one small comfort she clung to was that if her parents were involved with her daughter's abduction, they probably didn't mean Abby any harm.

But what if she was wrong? Obviously, they had completely different definitions of what constituted good and bad. Given the bizarre circumstances and their equally bizarre beliefs, could she trust that they wouldn't hurt Abby?

The possibility that they would harm Abby was too horrible for her to bear. She raised her chin and marched on. Better to tackle the obstacle in front of her. If the situation grew worse, she'd cross that bridge when she got to it.

As the ground squelched under her feet, she rounded the last bend in the driveway. She gasped at the house that came into view. It was much larger than she could have imagined.

How had she not realized this compound was here or that her parents were a part of it? It had taken her less than an hour to get here. Technically, it wasn't far from town. Yet she might as well have been on another planet. It had been pure luck that Jesse had the His Glory's Children map up on his monitor when she called him in to dinner, or she'd never have known where to look. Even then, her navigator had struggled to find the turnoff.

Standing alone in front of this massive white house, she realized how out of her depth she truly was. It was going to take a long time to search all those rooms, and that was assuming Abby was being held here at all.

She traipsed up the circular drive, which held an angel fountain in the center. It was dry, being the middle of winter, but someone had draped it in pine boughs and white Christmas lights. It would have been warm and welcoming if the experience at the gate hadn't been fresh in her mind.

Climbing the front steps was intimidating, but not as much as contemplating the heavy, carved wooden doors looming in front of her. A brass knocker in the shape of a large cross hung in the center of each door. She lifted the ring hanging from the bottom of one of them, but it opened before she had a chance to drop it back into place.

At first glance, the man before her appeared surprisingly normal. He wore a white, long-sleeved, button-down shirt, the sleeves of which he had rolled to the top of his forearms, and a pair of khaki slacks. His feet, she noticed, were clad in brown leather loafers.

He could have been mistaken for a traveling salesman, or middle management in any office across the country, until you looked at his eyes. They were pale blue—pale enough that they looked nearly silver in the overhead light. Their cold, sharp intensity made her want to take a step back.

"You must be Jackie. My name is Jeremiah Jones." Despite the introduction, he didn't move to shake her hand.

She straightened her shoulders. "I'm here to see my parents."

His thin lips formed a moue of disapproval. He stepped back reluctantly. "I'm aware. They are in the front sitting room."

"Thank you." She edged past him, then stood in the foyer waiting for him to indicate which direction to turn. The front entryway was as lavish as the walk up had indicated. Most of the floor was comprised of a black-and-tan tile carpet in a chevron pattern. Directly across from her was an elegant staircase that rose gracefully to the second floor. On either side of her were doorways leading into the rest of the house.

"This way." Jeremiah led her into a small sitting room. Mullioned windows faced the front of the house to her left, and a wall of built-in shelves stood to her right. Her parents sat with their backs toward the door, on a couch facing the fireplace across the room. Condensation ran down the two glasses of water placed on the table in front of them. Cordovan leather club chairs took up either side of the table, completing the conversation circle.

Her father rose and faced them when they entered. He wasn't a particularly tall man, but he had stature. She was surprised to discover he had a full head of white hair and a well-trimmed beard. Last time she'd seen him, it had still been more pepper than salt.

Jackie looked for some warmth or emotion from him, but his expression remained grim. The blue eyes she had inherited were distant and unreachable. He inclined his head. "Jackie."

She hadn't seen him for six years, and some part of her fantasized that his feelings toward her might have changed in the time they'd been apart, but his comportment disabused her of the notion.

"Father." Her gaze dropped to the woman twisted around and staring from her seat. "Mother."

A wisp of a smile crossed her mom's face, and her eyes held an undeniable sheen. Tears were caught in the fine web of lines cast from their corners. Regret and yearning filled Jackie's breast. It was the thread she was looking for. If she could get her mother alone, maybe they could make a real connection.

"Isn't this nice? An impromptu family reunion." Jeremiah slipped into one of the chairs and indicated Jackie should take the other. "We're very curious to find out what could be important enough that you had to see them tonight, at this late hour—especially after all this time."

With the first volley lobbed, he sat back and propped a foot on one knee, looking very much like a king in his castle. Jackie sank in the chair across from him, unsure of where to start. "I'm not sure what you've heard, but my daughter"—here, she addressed her parents—"your granddaughter, has gone missing." She returned her attention to Jeremiah, instinct demanding she kept her focus on the biggest threat in the room. "Unfortunately, the FBI agents don't have any leads and there haven't been any demands for a ransom."

"What a shame that this has happened." Jeremiah steepled his fingers in front of him and tapped his chin. "We were aware of the situation, of course, but not of the details and lack of progress in the case.

"Do you believe in God, Jackie?" He leaned forward, his gaze sharp. "Do you believe He is the Creator of all things?"

"Um," she stumbled, caught off guard by his intensity as much as the questions themselves. She struggled to pick her words carefully. "I believe that there is something greater than us. A higher power, if you will."

A sly grin had the corners of his mouth turning up. She shifted uncomfortably in her seat, feeling like she might have stumbled into an unseen trap. "'And God is faithful; He will not let you be tempted beyond what you can bear. But when you are tempted, He will also provide a way out so that you can endure it'. First Corinthians 10:13."

"Amen," her parents chimed, their perfectly synced voices sending shivers down her back.

Anger spiked through her system. Jackie doubted that God would sanction kidnapping children as a test of devotion. And frankly, if he did, she wanted no part of him or of a religion that worshipped him. However, that probably wasn't the response Jeremiah was hoping for when he quoted scripture. She decided to keep her mouth shut.

"In other words, He will not give you more than you can handle, but you must have faith, for He works in mysterious ways."

"I understood what you meant," she muttered.

He leaned back and regarded her with narrowed eyes. Whatever he'd been expecting from her, he appeared to be disappointed by her lack of reaction. An unsettling silence grew between them.

"I'm sorry, how rude of me. Would you like some water?" Not bothering to wait for her response, he snapped his fingers. Her mother practically jumped to her feet and scurried to a drink cart in the corner, which Jackie hadn't noticed previously. She returned with two glasses of water carefully balanced on coasters.

Jackie examined her mom as she bent at the knees and waist and reverently placed one of the glasses in front of him before putting Jackie's down on the table before her.

"Thanks, Mom," she whispered while her heart ached. Any half-baked plans that she had of enlisting her mother's help withered. If this had been Jeremiah's way of displaying her mom's full commitment and devotion to whatever society they had fashioned here, he had succeeded.

Jackie wondered if he had also given the order to remind Mary that she was to be the dutiful, silent, obedient wife put here to serve and fulfill the menfolk. Whatever the reason, she could see by the way her mom rejoined her father on the couch that it had been effective.

"Where were we?" Jeremiah asked. "Ah, yes, your daughter. Are you sure she didn't run away?"

He meant for the question to put her on the defensive. Jackie struggled to keep the stab of pain in her heart from showing on her face. "Yes. Abby would never do that. We have a very close relationship." She paused for half a beat. "We've had to."

Although her gaze never left his, she said the last sentence with a hint of bitterness. A small, spiteful part of her was satisfied to see her mom flinch from the corner of her eye.

"Listen here, Jackie…"—her father's face flushed with indignation— "if you hadn't been such a harlot, sullying our good name—"

"Tsk, tsk, tsk, such ugly language, Mark," Jeremiah admonished.

He gave Jackie a disapproving look, even as his expression held an edge of satisfaction. "Your last comment was insensitive. That's no way to honor your mother and father."

"I apologize," she responded, hoping her tone was properly contrite. Jackie counted to ten and reminded herself that it was easier to catch flies with honey than vinegar.

He inclined his head. "Good girl."

Her teeth ground at the phrase and the approval in his voice. What was it with the men in this cult talking to her like she was five?

He took a sip from his water glass before continuing. "And how did you expect coming here would help?"

"There was a woman in the store that talked to my daughter on the day Abby was abducted. She has ties to your... group, and I was wondering if she was involved somehow."

"This is outrageous!" Her father jumped to his feet. "After six years without any communication, how dare you come here and accuse us—"

"Mark." Jeremiah managed to infuse that single syllable with enough warning that it immediately halted his tirade. Her father abruptly sat; however, his face stayed an unhealthy shade of cardinal. Mary reached out to comfort him, but he shoved her hand away.

Jeremiah's expression frosted. "I hope you're not implying we've kidnapped your daughter."

A tremor shot through her body. Who knew what this man was capable of? She swallowed her misgivings and leveled a look at him. "You are the leader of this group, and as such, I can't imagine anything happens that you aren't aware of."

"You've chosen your words well. However, you didn't answer my question." He placed his empty water glass down with unnatural care. "I assure you that whoever you are referring to did not drive away with your daughter."

"I see I'm not the only one who can choose my words carefully."

His expression was glacial and sharp enough to cut glass. "We're done here. You may say your goodbyes to your parents, but I must insist that you be off the premises in the next fifteen minutes." After dropping his decree, he exited the room, looking fully confident that his will would be carried out.

She sprang to her feet. "What? No. You have my daughter! I demand to see her!" Fury and desperation flooded her system. Turning to her mother, she dropped to her knees. "Mom, please. This isn't right. Don't let them keep me away from my daughter."

Tears streamed down her mother's powdered cheeks, but she remained seated with her hands clasped and pressed against her lap.

"That's enough!" her father blustered. "I had hoped in the past six years that you would have learned some respect."

"You don't deserve respect! I know you had something to do with my daughter's disappearance, and I will do everything in my power to prove it. You think I was a willful girl back then? You haven't seen anything yet."

"*Out!*" Mark's face was red, his girth heaving with the force of his outrage. He shook his finger in her face. "And don't bother coming back. You are no daughter of mine."

Jackie's whole body trembled as she stalked toward the front entryway.

"Wait!" The desperation in her mother's voice stopped her as she opened the heavy door.

"Mary…" The warning in her father's voice was clear, but for the first time that Jackie could remember, Mary pressed on.

"Jackie, wait."

She faced her mother, surprised to find herself engulfed by her embrace. "'Trust in the Lord with all your heart and lean not on your own understanding; in all your ways submit to him, and he will make your paths straight.' Proverbs 26:25."

"Mom." Disappointment laced her voice. Why did she constantly hope for a connection that neither of her parents wanted?

Mary stepped away and gripped her hands, her expression intense. "Proverbs 26:25."

"Oh, Mom." She moved to dash the tears from her face, but her mother's grasp tightened until Jackie's fingers ached. She startled when a slip of paper was tucked into her palm but kept her face carefully neutral. Finally, Mary released her hands as Mark placed both hands on Mary's arms and yanked her away.

"Repent, then, and turn to God, so that he will forgive your sins," he intoned. "Only then will I look forward to once again calling you daughter." His fingertips were white, and Jackie hoped her mom wouldn't suffer too much for her actions.

"Goodbye, Mother."

Jackie didn't bother acknowledging her father, but couldn't resist the urge to look back at her mom from the front porch. Jeremiah stood on the staircase looking down on them from above.

Her heart ached at the resignation in her mother's drooped shoulders before the door was shut firmly in her face.

She didn't dare inspect the paper digging into her palm. Her fingers curled tighter as she began her journey down the driveway and back to the gate.

A spear of headlights and shouting drew her out of her daze as she approached the guardhouse. She shouldn't have been surprised to find Tom gripping the gate from the other side.

"Let me in, damn it!"

"Tom!"

The first guard was standing outside the gate with his feet spread wide and his gun held conspicuously in the crook of his arm. Kenny spun toward her. "It's time for you to leave—and take this asshole with you!"

"Jackie, are you okay?"

Define okay. "Yes, I'll be right out." Turning to Kenny, she held out her empty hand. "May I have my phone and keys, please?"

"Here." He smirked as he handed them to her. "Did you find what you were looking for?"

She ignored him and climbed into her car, taking care not to drop the slip of paper her mom had worked hard to give her.

A few blocks down the road, she drove to the shoulder and waited for Tom to park behind her. He wrenched the door open and dragged her out of the car before clutching her to his chest.

"*What the hell were you doing?*"

"I'm sorry," she mumbled. She breathed him in, enjoying the scent of soap and laundry detergent on his skin. His heart beat erratically beneath her cheek.

"I can't believe you did that. Do you have any idea how terrified I was? Mason has already called me. The whole task force has been out looking for you."

She drew back to arm's length and looked up into his face, willing him to understand. "I… I had to see their reactions when I asked them." Spinning away, she ran a hand through her hair. "I was hoping there might be some remnants of our relationship there. Something worth,"—she sighed—"worth salvaging."

He was quiet for a moment. "And, was there?"

"With my father? No." Jackie hung her head, feeling the truth of her words. "But with my mother?" She held her hand out and revealed the small scrap of paper lying in her palm. "Maybe."

"What is that?"

"I don't know. I didn't dare open it while I was still on their compound." Carefully, she unfolded the paper. She pondered the small, black squares and lines crammed on the tiny slip. She tilted her head. "It's not in any language that I can understand."

"Here, let me see." Tom took the paper and smoothed it flat on the hood of her car, the headlights providing enough ambient light to see. His brow wrinkled before he rotated it ninety degrees. "It could be a map."

"Really?" Jackie looked at it from the new angle. "Yes, you might be right. There! Doesn't that line look like where the front gate is?" She traced her finger up one of the lines that ran perpendicular to the first. "And, here's the bend in the driveway as you walk up to the house...."

"Which would make this rectangle the main house, right?"

"That looks about right."

"Assuming that's what this is, what is this over here?" Tom pointed to a small square set in the middle of what would be the woods.

Hope surged in her breast. "I have no idea, but it's worth checking out."

"I agree." He blew out a breath. "I hate to say this, but before we do that, we have to take this back to the authorities. It will go a lot better for us if we can do this legally, with a warrant."

Every molecule in Jackie's body was screaming for her to drive back and search the entire compound and premises. However, after seeing their security measures firsthand, she knew she wouldn't get very far before being kicked out. Not to mention, her actions could make it harder for the authorities to gain access in the long run.

Her head fell back, and she looked at the sky for a moment before saying words she hated to admit. "You're right."

CHAPTER SEVENTEEN

TOM WAS THANKFUL that Agent Reyes—Marta— refrained from giving Jackie a full dressing down when they returned.

Still, the remarks she did make were effective. Jackie slumped when Marta had said, "There goes the element of surprise. Let's hope that if your daughter is there, they don't try to move her. You realize they are probably calling their lawyers as we speak."

Jackie apologized, and Marta soon took pity on her. "Don't worry, all it means is that we'll have to act quickly. The good news is, this map, the circumstances in which it was delivered—as well as by whom—will be sufficient enough proof to get the warrant I've been asking for. I don't agree with your method, but overall, you did a good job."

"Thank you, Marta," Jackie said.

"Is there anything else you'd like to report?"

"I'm not sure, yet." Jackie hesitated. "I feel like I missed something, but I can't place my finger on it."

Marta held her silence for half a beat before saying, "Give it some space. Sometimes, when we've had an emotionally traumatic experience, our mind moves to protect itself. You've had a series of them in the last"—she glanced at her watch and grimaced—"twelve hours. Damn, I can't believe it's nearly midnight."

She said the last sentence under her breath, and Tom wondered at the implications. He knew that the first twenty-four hours after a child went missing were the most crucial. That window of time was nearly half over, and he felt like they'd made little progress.

Rolling her shoulders back, Agent Reyes shook herself alert. "Why don't you try and get some rest? Perhaps the answers you're trying to remember will present themselves when you're refreshed."

"There's no way I could sleep."

She nodded in sympathy, unsurprised by Jackie's answer. "That's fine. Then find something else to do. Go make a pot of tea."

"I can do that. Would you like some?"

The older woman brightened. "I thought you'd never ask."

Jackie sighed. "Thank you. I'm sorry for sneaking out the way I did."

"Splitting our attention in a case like this wasn't ideal. However, if I were in your shoes, I can't say I'd handle the situation any differently. That being said, please don't do it again. I'd hate to have to arrest you." Despite the understanding in her expression, her tone was steely.

Marta focused on the young man tapping on his computer. "Agent Townsend, after this assignment, we're going to review our information protocols."

"Yes, ma'am." Agent Townsend's voice was glum.

"Please, don't punish Jesse," Jackie protested. "It wasn't his fault."

Marta patted Jackie's hand. "If you could, I'd like a teaspoon of honey with my tea, please." She quickly dialed a number into her phone and moved across the room, speaking rapidly under her breath.

Mason walked over to them. "I should be pissed at both of you."

"I couldn't let her go alone."

"Don't worry, I understand why you ran off like that. I know what Marta said, but if you feel the need to go against her orders, promise me you'll tell me next time."

"You got it."

Mason nodded toward Marta, who was still working her magic

on the phone. "If anybody can convince a judge to sign a warrant in the dead of night, she can."

"I believe it." Tom followed Jackie into the kitchen and found her standing over the stove talking to herself. "Are you... praying?"

"What? No. I'm going over something my mom said right before I left."

"What's that?"

"She quoted a passage from the Bible. 'Trust in the Lord with all your heart and lean not on your own understanding; in all your ways submit to him, and he will make your paths straight.'"

"What could it mean?"

She put the teakettle on the burner. "At first, I suspected she was encouraging me to 'submit' to the teachings of their cult and join them, but after mulling it over, I'm not sure."

"Why not?"

"Because, at the end of the quote, she cited it as a passage from Proverbs 26:25—twice—but I'm pretty sure that's not right. I mean, it's been a while since I've read the Bible, but I could have sworn that came from a different part of Proverbs."

"That's easy enough to check." Tom removed his phone from his pocket. "Proverbs 26:25, you say?" He put it into the search engine. "You're right, it doesn't match. This one says, 'A malicious man disguises himself with his lips, but in his heart he harbors deceit. Though his speech is charming, do not believe him, for seven abominations fill his heart.' What the hell is that supposed to mean?"

"I'm not sure how she wants me to interpret it, but the malicious man disguising himself with charming speech is probably referring to Jeremiah himself."

"Or your father," he suggested.

She paused. "No, not even my mother could stretch the truth that far. My father was definitely not trying to deceive me with charming words."

Tom regarded this information, then reached for a couple of

mugs and set them on the counter. "I'll buy that. If Jeremiah is the charming deceiver, then what are these 'seven abominations'?"

She pondered the question as she took the honey down from the cupboard. "There are seven major sins. How does that pertain to this situation, though? Unless… you don't think my mother was trying to tell me he has seven children, do you?"

Doubt filled his mind. "Would he regard children as sinful?"

She rubbed the spot between her eyebrows. "Honestly, I don't know what he would consider sinful. The man's views are clearly extreme. Talking to him felt like… I can't describe it." He watched her struggle to find the right words. "Oily. Sinister. Maybe… evil?"

"Evil how, exactly?"

She sighed. "Wicked. He looked at me as if I were a worm and he enjoyed watching me writhe on the hook."

A terrifying possibility came to Tom, but he loathed saying it out loud. Unfortunately, Jackie was too good at reading him. "What? What crossed your mind?"

"Could it mean she only has seven days?"

"Oh, God." Her face became bone-white. "I hope we're wrong about that one."

"Me too." He glanced at the quote displayed on his phone. "There has to be a reason your mom felt it was important to reference this particular proverb."

The teakettle whistled, insisting they return to the task at hand. Together they poured and doctored everybody's tea. She picked up her mug and one with a teaspoon of honey inside. "I should inform Agent Reyes of what we're talking about."

"Agreed. She might have a different angle to consider." *Preferably one not as grim.*

CHAPTER EIGHTEEN

THE NEXT MORNING, Randy woke up splayed face down on the bed with his head under the pillow. His mouth tasted like a cheap distillery. Every joint in his body ached from the awkward position he'd slept in. As he rolled out of bed, nausea climbed his throat and he had to fight the urge to puke.

With great effort, he managed to sit on the edge of the bed. Propping his elbows on his knees, he stared at the frayed and stained condition of the brown carpet between his feet and debated whether any vomit would get noticed on the ugly floor. Hell, it might even be an improvement.

He held his pounding head between his hands. What had he done?

He'd jeopardized his freedom by violating his parole for a couple bottles of cheap vodka. Maybe his parole officer wouldn't find out. At least there wasn't any evidence to get rid of, other than his blood alcohol content.

"Shit," he said then regretted it. Even the sound of his own voice was too harsh for his sensitive head. Jackie's new guy, what was his name? Tom? Tom had definitely done him a solid by removing the bottles from his room. He and some other woman—he remembered that she was hot—had been here asking him questions.

As if he knew anything about his missing daughter. He was a

jackass, sure, but not like that. He'd never harm a kid, especially not his own. Indignation filled his chest before the memory of her being abducted deflated it again.

He had to do something, dammit! Didn't he? Granted, he'd never been a part of her life before, but he wasn't going to let her disappear, either. His heart twisted in pain at the memory of seeing her up on the stage in her little elf costume. She'd been incredibly proud and happy ringing that bell.

He could only imagine how much patience it would have taken to have her practice that in the house all day. The mere thought of the racket made his hangover send shafts of pain through his brain.

Jackie was a bigger saint than he'd ever given her credit for.

He dragged his ass into the bathroom and started the shower. The first thing he should to do was pull himself together, then he'd figure out what to do for his little girl.

Ten minutes later, he stepped out of the steamy room in a towel and rummaged through the dresser for a pair of boxers. The pounding in his skull had retreated to a dull roar. He knew from experience that a couple cups of coffee and some greasy breakfast food would take care of the rest.

After a brief search, he found the remote to the beat-up TV and flipped it to a news station. A school photo of Abby took up the whole screen. It was the sort of picture gracing mantles all across the country, with gap-toothed children dressed in their best outfits, sitting in front of an ever-present blue backdrop. The shock of it was a punch to the gut, and it took him a second to tune in to what the reporter was saying.

"The search continues for Abby Davis, a six-year-old girl who was snatched from a store while Christmas shopping with her mother in Bath, Maine, yesterday."

A second photo took up the right side of the screen. It was a mugshot of a woman in her fifties. The image changed to one of her standing with a group of people and holding a sign saying, "Sinners Repent!"

"Police are looking for this woman as a person of interest in the case. She is believed to have ties to the group His Glory's Children—an ultraconservative religious group operating north of Union, Maine. She was last seen at the store talking with Abby Davis on the day of the abduction.

"If you have seen either one of these individuals, please contact the police hotline." The number flashed across the screen as the reporter paused half a beat then jumped into her next segue. "And now, let's talk about sports! How about those Pats, Dan?"

Son of a bitch! Randy switched the television off and tossed the remote down on the bed. He remembered how religious Jackie's parents were. Hell, he'd grown up in the same church community that Jackie had, which was why he'd been allowed to date her in the first place.

Had things changed that much since he'd left? Did the fundamentalist church mutate into the HGC cult? The possibility didn't seem so far-fetched. But, abducting children? That was way more extreme than Randy would have thought they'd go.

On second thought, remembering how viciously they had ostracized their daughter for getting pregnant, he wouldn't put it past them. Guilt gnawed at his insides when he considered the role he'd played, but he shoved the familiar feeling aside. This wasn't about him or Jackie—or their past. This was about getting Abby back.

Judging by the news report, it sounded like the authorities already knew where she was. They were just too chickenshit to go get her. But he wasn't.

For once in his life, he was going to do something right. He wiped his palms down the front of his jeans, already sweaty from contemplating his half-cocked plan. Before he did anything, he was going to require more liquid courage.

Throwing a dingy T-shirt over his head, he snagged his keys, barely remembering to lock the door behind him. His hands shook as he slid into the driver's seat and reversed out of the parking lot.

The clerk at the liquor store conspicuously checked the time, eyeing him sideways as he rung up Randy's purchase.

"Yeah, yeah, yeah, be glad you're making money off me," Randy grumbled. He reached into his pocket and handed him a crumpled twenty-dollar bill. It was his last one.

"I'm sorry?" the clerk asked, not bothering to hide the censure in his tone.

Randy sneered. "I bet you are, working in a place like this." He took his change and snatched the large plastic bottle of vodka off the counter.

Stepping out of the store, he took a good look at his beater of a car. It was the only one he could afford after getting released from prison, and even then, the dealer probably fleeced him.

It was an ugly shade of mustard yellow except where it was dented and rusted. The trunk latch was held shut with a plastic tie because it had broken a few days after Randy had driven the car off the lot. The damn thing liked to guzzle gas like a thirsty man sitting on a barstool at five in the morning. However, despite these flaws, it had two good points working in its favor.

It was heavy and it had a big grille.

CHAPTER NINETEEN

A FEW MINUTES past six a.m., someone pounded on the bedroom door.

"Son of a bitch," Tom grumbled. Jackie stirred, but he tucked the covers up over her. "No, you stay here. I'll get it."

He walked to the door and flung it open. "What?"

"The warrant came through. Marta finally got through to some poor judge who probably got tired of listening to her and wanted to go to bed. We're heading out in five." Mason's voice was still chilly but was more conciliatory than it had been last night.

Tom retrieved his jeans off the floor as Mason stood in the doorway and gave him the update. He shrugged on the flannel he'd worn the day before and stepped into his boots.

"I'm coming, too," Jackie said from behind him.

"Are you sure? I think you should—"

"No, I'm coming, too." She flung the covers off, revealing the fact she was clad only in a pair of panties and T-shirt. Apparently, it didn't matter to her. Tom supposed something as mundane as modesty wasn't even on the priority list when it came to getting Abby back.

Mason had the decency to turn his head while she put her jeans on. He faced the doorframe and said, "Fine, but you're staying in the car."

She continued dressing and pulled her knee-high boots on and zipped them up.

Ready, Tom rubbed a hand over his face, scratching at the stubble. They'd both been exhausted by the time they'd fallen into bed. None of them were working on more than a couple hours of sleep.

"I'll keep an eye on her," he assured his friend. He knew it was a big risk to let them come, but there was no way he was going to be excluded.

Mason's eyes were blood-shot but steady. "I'm not sure if that's better or worse." He spun on his heel. "Truck's leaving in two minutes."

They backed out of the driveway right on time. He shouldn't have been surprised to see Olivia in the passenger seat when they'd come out of the house. She handed them each a cup of coffee. "Here. Be careful, it's hot."

"You're an angel," he told her, then took a bracing sip, disregarding the bite of heat on his tongue.

She looked over at Jackie. "How are you holding up?"

Jackie wrapped her hands around the warm cup and inhaled deeply. "She's there. I can feel it."

"If she is, we'll get her." Mason glanced at her in the rearview mirror, a note of warning in his voice. "However, I was serious back there in the house. You are to stay in the car until we're sure. Got it?"

"Got it." Jackie pursed her lips and looked out the window. Tom leaned back in his seat, wondering how closely she planned on following the rules.

Mason must have come to the same conclusion because he hazarded another glance in the mirror before turning his full attention back to the road. Olivia patted his knee.

"What does the warrant encompass?" Tom asked.

"It's a full warrant, including the house and grounds."

He grunted in satisfaction. "Good. I'll be curious to find out what that square was in the woods."

"Me too." Mason paused, as though debating whether he should go further. "It could be nothing."

"Could be. Might not be."

"There's gonna be a lot of people surveilling the property. Agent Reyes called in backup from the surrounding towns, including a SWAT unit. We won't go in until they're all assembled."

"What?" That captured Jackie's attention. "We're all going to gather outside the gate and inform them we're there? I have an idea. While we're at it, let's send them a text and tell them we're coming."

Tom did a double-take. He'd never heard her voice laced with such sarcasm and contempt. "Jackie, you have every right to be frustrated, but—"

"But, what?" Her tone was brittle. "This whole time I've been expected to sit on my hands and wait, stay calm, make dinner...." She let out a snort that sounded anything but funny. "The one time I dared to do something constructive, I had to sneak out of my own house and then got in trouble for it! Mind you, that's after I managed to procure the only solid clue we've had in this case. This is my *daughter*, Tom. How could you possibly understand what this feels like?"

Her words sliced him to the bone. No, deeper. To the heart.

Silence descended in the cab, and Mason and Olivia exchanged a look. Mason opened his mouth, but Olivia shook her head slightly and he closed it again.

He stared back at Jackie, whose face was filling with horror and regret. "Tom, I—"

He raised a hand. Some part of him understood that she hadn't meant those words, but knowing that didn't get rid of the pain filling his chest. "It's fine, Jackie. Let's hope she's there."

Tears fell down her cheeks, but for once, he didn't try to wipe them from her face.

*

Mason parked on the side of the road behind a police car. "I don't see the SWAT vehicle yet. I'm going to find Agent Reyes and see what the plan is." He opened the door.

"Hey," Olivia said, calling him back in. She leaned over the center console and gave him a kiss. "You be careful."

"Always." Tom watched as Mason caressed her cheek. "You're not getting rid of me that easy."

"Better not," she replied. Despite her light tone, her eyes held concern. Tom gazed out the window as Mason kissed her nose then climbed out of the cab.

"Tom, can I talk to you for a second?" Mason said.

"Sure." He joined his friend at the back of the truck.

"How are you holding up?" Mason asked.

Tom kicked the back tire. "She's under a lot of stress."

"You are, too." He sighed. "We all are."

"True, but she's right. It's different for her." He leaned against the bed of the truck. "Honestly, I'm surprised she hasn't had an outburst before this."

"Me too." Mason slapped him on the back. "It still doesn't make it easy to bear. You can talk to me."

"Thanks." And Tom meant it. It had been a while since he'd had that kind of friendship in his life, but it felt good. Even when the circumstances were bad.

"All right, I'm going to find the boss and see what's happening. Make sure everyone remains here."

"You got it." Tom stayed put as Mason moved away. The stretch of road right in front of the compound's front gate had been closed down to one lane, and two cops directed traffic on both ends. The group of cars they were parked in was located inside the area that had been cordoned off. A handful of news crews gathered just beyond the barrier.

Inside the zone, he spotted nearly a dozen cop cars from three different jurisdictions, including the sheriff's office. He surmised that the FBI agents must have arrived in the gray, nondescript Ford sedans parked closest to the front gate.

He was unsettled when the paramedics arrived in their ambulance and set up toward the back of the group, closer to the area's perimeter. He could see them eating fast-food breakfast sandwiches in the cab and wondered if they were starting their shift or ending it.

Despite the number of people, the area was mostly silent. Someone must have given an order for everyone to approach without sirens.

"Hey, can I talk to you?" Jackie stood beside him.

Tom jumped, surprised that she'd caught him off guard. He stuffed his hands in his pockets to keep from reaching for her. "Yeah."

Tears brimmed, but she blinked them back, leaving her eyelashes spiky. Even hurt and pissed, he couldn't help being drawn to her. He'd felt that way ever since his first day of work at the café.

"I'm sorry. I realize how much you love Abby and that you'd do anything you could for her." She held one arm around her waist while a fisted hand covered her mouth. "What am I going to do if she's not here? Or if something has happened to her?"

"Shh. Shh, honey." Tom held her. Hot tears drenched the front of his shirt.

Her arms wound around him. He couldn't do anything more for her but hold on through the emotional storm, so that's what he did. Tears pricked the insides of his lids, and he cried with her.

By the time Jackie calmed down, he wasn't sure if he'd been holding her for two minutes or twenty. He dropped a kiss upon her head before releasing her. "Feel better?"

"No." She looked up at him with drenched eyes. "Not really. Not until I get Abby back."

"I understand." He would have continued, but a rusty, orange behemoth of a car barreled through the traffic stop. "Watch out!" He pushed her to the side of the road and watched as the vehicle careened past.

"Someone is going to get hurt!" Jackie exclaimed.

"Who the hell was that?" Olivia bounded out of the front seat and joined them.

"I'm not sure. I could be wrong, but it looked a lot like Randy," Tom said.

Jackie released a sound of pure exasperation. "That asshole is going to ruin everything!" She sprinted toward the gate.

"Jackie, wait!" She didn't stop. Instead, she put her head down and pumped her legs even faster. "Dammit, woman," he growled as he took off after her.

"Guys! You're supposed to stay in the car!" Olivia shouted. "For fuck's sake." He could hear her footsteps pounding the pavement behind him.

A great crashing boom reverberated through the air, and for a split second, everybody froze, then jumped back into motion twice as fast. People all around them were waving their arms and shouting.

"Stop right there!"

"Watch out, he's backing up!"

"Put your hands up!"

Another thunderous clatter rent the air, followed by the loud squealing of hinges protesting.

Jackie, Tom, and Olivia all drew up on the scene breathless. A few law enforcement officers were being helped to their feet where they must have dived for cover. Some of the cops had drawn their pistols and were approaching the vehicle from the side, shouting at the driver to get out and put his hands up.

Whether the driver heard them was hard to say, because he was backing up for a third time. The engine revved in warning, and he sped toward the tall iron gates, which were already damaged and struggling to stay upright.

Boom!

One of the gate's sides finally fell to the ground. The car flew forward.

"Go, go, go!" Agent Reyes shouted into her radio. "The bastard has taken any semblance of control out of our hands. Get in there before he ruins everything!"

"Yes, ma'am," the radio squawked.

Jackie must have heard her and seen her chance because she sprinted past the chaos and slipped into the woods. Tom stayed right behind her.

Something that sounded like a firecracker reverberated through the trees on their right. "Duck," Tom yelled.

Jackie lowered her head but didn't slow down.

"Jackie, wait!"

"I can't stop, Tom. I've got to get to her." Desperation infused her words even as she struggled for air.

"Jackie. I get it." He reached forward and grasped her arm, then used their momentum to drag them to the ground.

They both lay panting in the woods, plumes from their breath fogging the air around them. "Tom! Let me go! We have to get to her." Jackie struggled under his weight, pounding his chest.

He slammed a hand over her mouth and hissed, "Jackie, stop!"

She stilled. Her eyes were wide and her pulse thrummed in her throat as her body struggled to stay oxygenated.

He leaned down and carefully placed a finger to the tragus of her ear. "Somebody is shooting at us," he whispered. "I'm going to remove my hand from your mouth, but you have to stay quiet. Understood?"

She nodded.

"Good. Keep your head down while I try to figure out where we are in relation to the map."

She nodded again, clearly no longer worried he was trying to stop her. This time, she regarded him with absolute trust. He removed his hand from her mouth, carefully raised his head, and scanned the trees around them. Another gunshot rang out, but it was farther to the right and pointed away from them.

He retraced their run through the woods in his mind and tried to calculate the shots' trajectory. Leaning down, he whispered in her ear again. "We're going to head away from the sound, but not so far that we run back into the driveway. Let me take the lead. Try to step where I step and follow as quickly and quietly as possible."

"Okay." She copied the way he rose to a crouch and ran hunched over until they could duck behind a tree trunk.

He'd gone into what he personally referred to as "warrior mode." Individual sights and sounds were weighed and cataloged by threat level in his mind. He gestured with his hand for her to get down farther, then peered out from behind the trunk. After ascertaining that the coast looked clear, he counted down with his fingers from three then sprinted to the next large tree.

From there, he could see a boulder. It would make a great place to take shelter, for them or somebody lying in wait. Not wanting to chance it, he whispered, "Stay here for a second and be quiet. Don't argue," he cut her off when she opened her mouth. "I'm going to make sure someone isn't hiding behind that rock over there, and then I'll wave you over."

Relief washed over her. "Okay."

He pressed a kiss to her mouth then ran toward the boulder. Creeping around the rocky face, he heard the soft scrape of someone's shoe and considered his options. It wasn't the first time he'd been at a disadvantage in a fight, but that didn't mean he liked it.

No gun, no knife. For a moment, he regretted falling out of the habit of always being prepared for battle. Then he remembered that had only happened because his life for the last few years had been happy and safe.

He hoped those years hadn't made him soft.

Not that he had a choice here. Tom cast about for anything he could use as a weapon.

The stick he spotted was a little longer than his arm and nearly as thick. It wasn't the best weapon in the world, but it wasn't the worst, either. He hefted it in his hands and assessed the weight. There would be no practice swings.

With soft footsteps, he rounded the corner right as Jackie quietly called out, "Tom?"

Shit!

The man was sighting down the barrel of his gun toward her voice. With two big steps, he swung the branch with everything he had, putting his full weight into it. The gun went off, blasting the air with sound, right as the wood in his hand connected to the back of the man's head.

The crunch of his skull sounded like walnut shells cracking. Tom winced. He felt no satisfaction at what he'd done. "Jackie!"

Half a second of pure terror passed before her tremulous voice responded, "I'm fine."

He rushed over to her, running his hands over her head and hair, down her shoulders and arms, desperate to verify she was unharmed. "What part of 'be quiet' didn't you understand?"

"I'm sorry. I-I didn't fully understand the consequences until I heard the shot." She bit her lip, shocked. "It was close. I felt the air rush past my cheek."

Tom closed his eyes and thanked the universe for sparing her. "Please promise me you will follow directions next time?"

"I will," she vowed.

"Let's go. The square on the map should be up this way." He took a few steps then stopped. "Stay down."

Jackie sent him a sheepish look and folded down until she was half her height.

He nodded with approval. "Better. Let's go."

*

The ground became more slippery the farther they trekked into the woods. The leaves were slick with damp, and piles of snow squatted at the base of trunks and shrubs, hiding roots. Small rocks and branches lay in wait, eager to twist ankles.

They slowed and carefully picked their way through the trees, brushing aside barren branches and startling a few squirrels. Jackie could still hear a commotion in the direction of the gate, but it was muffled and felt disconnected from what they were doing.

Tom paused, lowering himself behind a fallen log. His hand raised in a closed fist, indicating she should hold her position. It was such a natural motion that it didn't seem odd at all to Jackie that he had slipped back into combat training.

In fact, the only time he'd looked truly scared was when the gunshot had gone off and he wasn't sure if it had hit her. She shook her head, not wanting to focus on what a close call that had been. She suspected they'd both have plenty of nightmares about it later.

Luckily, she didn't have to wait long for him to tell her why they'd stopped.

"I see a shadow between the trees up there but can't make it out from this angle."

"Should we go around?" she asked.

He scanned the area in front of him. "Negative. Hold position while I scout the area. Whatever you do, stay radio silent."

Hearing him slip into full soldier mode caused alarm, but a moment later he turned to her and blinked. "Sorry. Do you have any questions?"

"Tom?" She raised a hand and cupped his face. "Please, stay in the present with me. I can't do this without you."

"It's under control." He tightened his jaw in grim determination. "Don't worry."

Leaning forward, she pressed her lips gently to his, letting him feel the warmth of her breath.

Tension eased from his shoulders. He gazed down at her and stroked her cheek. "Jackie, it's okay, I promise. Do me a favor: don't call out for me while I'm gone, understand?"

She grimaced. "Understood."

After another moment, he slipped away. He was silent enough that, even though she knew he was there, she couldn't tell where exactly he was.

With a sigh, she crouched and propped her back against a tree trunk, resigned to waiting. The bark was scratchy and familiar. Forest sounds gradually filtered into her consciousness. Squirrels scrabbled up trees, their claws clicking and scraping as they hunted for nuts. A woodpecker punctuated the air with its insistent knocking. Dead leaves rustled with unseen bugs as they went about their daily errands.

The scene would have been idyllic if the circumstances had been less dire.

Even as the idea crossed her mind, she knew that wasn't wholly correct. Nature was the one place she'd always been able to find God—in whatever way she imagined Him as a concept—and that couldn't be diminished or destroyed by the machinations or hubris of humans.

A twig snapped behind her, thrusting her back into the present. "It's me. I didn't want to startle you."

"What did you find?"

Tom's hesitation made her throat close. "You have to promise me that you're not going to do anything reckless."

"Oh, God…." She sank to her knees.

"No, no, Jackie…." He knelt in front of her. "She's alive. I saw her in the room, sitting on the floor. There are other children there with her, and two armed guards posted at the front and back doors."

Tears rushed unbidden as sweet relief flowed through her system. The only two words she'd been desperate to hear were *she's alive*. Everything else could be figured out.

"I barely managed to slip away unnoticed. They had a third guard standing sentry in the woods, but I took him out. Now, I have his gun." He held the hunting rifle up for her to see.

She was surprised to find she recognized it as the one belonging to the gate guard. "The last time I saw that gun, it was being held by a guy who was big and mean."

"Trust me, he was." His smile was feral. "But so am I."

A glint of something dangerous shifted in the depths of his gaze, but Jackie found it rather comforting. "Can we get my daughter?"

"Yes, follow me."

They circled the structure and stopped when they had a clear view of the front door. "What is this place?" Jackie asked as they crouched.

"I think it used to be a one-room hunting cabin. It looks like they're holding all the kids here."

"Just our luck." She shifted her weight. "How are we going to get past the guards?"

He looked at her sharply. "We aren't. I am."

"Outpost One, this is Home Base, come in, over." A sound of a walkie-talkie interrupted their conversation, and the guard they were watching raised one to his mouth.

"Home Base, this is Outpost One. Go ahead."

"Be advised. You may have heard a disturbance at the gate. State parties are at Home Base. Keep the innocents in full lockdown and stay vigilant. Over."

"Copy that. Over." The guard replaced the walkie talkie in his belt and shifted his rifle a little closer.

Kenny whooped. "You hear that, Dylan? Our Lord is testing our resolve! Hallelujah!"

"Shut up, Kenny. Asshole. Working with you has been my test this whole time."

Tom snorted in humor, and she wondered how he could remain calm given the circumstances. Although, after having to deal with Kenny herself, she could certainly relate to the guard named Dylan.

"Hey! That's not very nice." Kenny's voice had become petulant. "I'm going to tell Father Jeremiah."

"Whatever," Dylan said under his breath, but his face had blanched at the threat.

A child's wail floated out of the window, and Dylan grimaced. "Dammit, Kenny. Keep those kids quiet!"

"Why do I gotta do it? You're guarding them, too!"

"Because I have seniority. Get in there and shut them up."

Tom and Jackie heard a door slam, then Kenny yelling, "You kids behave. No, move away from him. How many times do I have to tell you to keep your hands to yourself? That's it, come here. You're standing in this corner, and you are standing over here."

It was Jackie's turn to snicker. Wrangling one six-year-old was tough, but a whole roomful of children? People underestimated how hard staying home and raising kids could be.

Dylan glanced toward the door in disgust, and in that instant, Tom shot up and rushed him. The guard didn't even get a chance to see his assailant before he was lying face down in the mud, weaponless.

Tom held the other man in a chokehold until the guard's eyes rolled up into the back of his head. The whole thing took less than three minutes.

She stepped out of the woods and looked down at the guard at her feet. "Wow. You're good."

"You ain't seen nothing yet," Tom assured her. He moved to the edge of the window and cautiously peered in. Jackie stood beside him with her back pressed against the cabin wall. She could hear the kids inside complaining that they were hungry.

"Wait here. I'm going to get him when he comes out."

"All right." Tom moved toward the other side of the cabin. It was hard for her to resist going in and comforting them. The urge to have her arms around Abby consumed her.

"Hey, wha—" It was the only sound Kenny made before his head hit the side of the wall. Moments later, Tom came jogging back around the corner. "Ready?"

"More than anything."

"Let's go."

Jackie rushed through the door, her heart pounding in her throat. "Abby? Abby!"

"Mommy!"

All she saw was a head of blonde hair before it launched at her. "Oh, baby! My baby! Are you hurt?" She peppered kisses all over her daughter's face and brushed her hair back, noting the long and white frilly dress she wore. "I've missed you so much!"

"Mommy!" All the tension and fear from the last day and a half rushed out of Abby on a wail. Jackie squeezed her little body closer, rubbing her back.

"Shh, honey. Mommy is here." Tears seeped out from under her closed lids as she rocked her daughter. "I'm here."

Tom's strong arms hugged them both. The three of them took a moment to simply hold each other before Abby wiggled. "Hi, Tom-tom! Did you come to rescue me?"

"Damn straight, kid. Your mom and I both did."

Abby reached for Tom, and tears fell down his cheeks. He gathered her in his arms. "Hey, Sprout."

She laid her head on his shoulder. "I love you, Tom."

He choked. "I love you, too, Abby."

Never one to stand still, Abby raised her head and pressed her hands to his cheeks. "Can you please help my friends?"

At her daughter's request, Jackie realized she'd momentarily forgotten the other children. A handful of them was gathered around, their ages ranging from three to eight years old. They were all dressed in similar pristine white dresses or tunics and pants.

"Hello," she said. The children crowded around her and Tom, their little faces clean and curious. Thankfully, all of them appeared to be unharmed. "Who's ready to go see their parents?"

"Father Jones only lets us see Mommy and Daddy when we learn our passages," one little boy said. "He pretends to be nice, but he's scary."

A chorus of "I want to see my mommy and daddy," sounded throughout the cabin.

Jackie regarded them, realization dawning. Was Jeremiah Jones separating the children from their parents as a means of indoctrinating them? Her heart ached as she contemplated the long road to recovery that lay ahead for all of the kids. She brushed a hand down her daughter's back. But at least they'd have the opportunity to heal.

Tom shifted Abby's weight into one arm and took his phone out to call the authorities. Jackie cringed when she realized she'd left her own phone back in the car. Once again, she'd run into danger ill-prepared, exactly like the previous night.

Tom raised an eyebrow at her then winked. "Don't worry. I'll always have your back."

She wrapped an arm around him and Abby. "I know."

CHAPTER TWENTY

THAT NIGHT ON the evening news, Tom and Jackie watched as all of the members of His Glory's Children were handcuffed and escorted off the compound.

A stunning, titian-haired reporter stood with the ravaged gates framed behind her. "This was the dramatic scene today as Randy Peterson, the father of a missing child, rammed his car into the front gate of what some have called a cult known as His Glory's Children.

"This reckless display set off a chain of events that eventually led to the rescue of Abby Davis, who had been missing since yesterday. Jeremiah Jones, the leader of the religious group, was arrested.

"According to anonymous sources who are close to the family, it's unclear what consequences Randy Peterson will face. He is a parolee who was recently released from jail for good behavior but was under strict terms, which included remaining sober for the duration of his parole. Witnesses say that was not the case as he repeatedly drove his 1978 Malibu Chevy into the iron gates at the compound."

"What will happen to Randy, I wonder?" Jackie asked. She considered what he'd done. It had been foolish and reckless, yet she was so, so grateful to him.

"I heard his parole officer tell him he was going back to jail."

She blew a heavy breath out, feeling conflicted. Up until today, she would have fought tooth and nail against joint custody. Even after Mason warned her that the courts usually decided in favor of keeping children with both biological parents, she'd been hoping to keep Abby away from him.

But now?

She couldn't exactly condone his actions. They'd put every first responder in the area at risk. One officer had a broken wrist from diving out of the car's way. Yet, would the outcome have been the same if he hadn't forced his way in? They did have a warrant in hand to search the property, but with three armed guards surrounding the compound's children, what would it have taken to get them away?

She shuddered imagining those children being used as hostages—or worse—caught in crossfire.

"If it makes a difference, I believe he is sincerely trying to get sober and become a better man," Tom said.

Jackie was surprised. "You do?"

"I do." Tom shrugged. "There are going to be setbacks. Even fairly well-adjusted people would have struggled to deal with the situation we found ourselves in these last few days. I did. And, he was still early in his transition out of jail, trying to acclimate to his new life."

He propped himself up on his elbow and looked down at her. His hand lay flat and warm on her stomach. "I'm not saying he should get a free pass for what he did today, or a blank check for anything that happens tomorrow, but his heart was in the right place and he was trying to help. That has to count for something."

She sighed. "I suppose it does." She paused. "I still don't feel comfortable leaving Abby alone with him, but we can start slowly with chaperoned visits once he's out of jail. We'll give him a chance to earn his redemption."

"That's a good place to start."

The images flickering across the screen caught their attention once more. The camera crews had certainly outdone themselves, capturing Randy's mad crash into the gate, the subsequent chaos, Jeremiah Jones as he exited the large white house and walked down the front steps, her own parents as they peered out of the back window of a cop car, her mother openly weeping and her father sitting stoically, no remorse apparent on his face.

She was still reeling from the reasons her father had given for kidnapping her daughter. He'd wanted to raise Abby in the cult, under Jeremiah's teachings. After seeing the news article about their café, he'd promised his leader a new follower. When Jackie confronted him during his arrest, he'd spat in her face and told her she was living in sin, that his granddaughter deserved better.

Jackie knew that the door to her father would forever remain closed, but she couldn't muster up the energy to regret it. Not after what he'd done. Her mother, on the other hand, didn't know about the plans until too late. She hoped, in time, she'd be able to reach out to her. After Mary helped find and rescue Abby, the possibility didn't seem far-fetched.

She shoved her musings away, knowing they would keep until later. "This is my favorite part." Sitting up, she leaned against Tom. The camera lingered on the three of them standing outside the gate, Abby between them. Jackie decided it wasn't bad having the crews there to capture that.

On the other hand... "Can you tell me how you knew where to look for the children?" the reporter asked, thrusting a microphone in Jackie's face.

All the color drained from her cheeks, emphasizing the bags under her eyes caused by worry and lack of sleep. She stood there like a deer caught in headlights, only this time they were floodlights. "I, well... you see..." She cast her gaze off to the side, desperately looking for help out of the interview.

On the couch, Tom chuckled. She hit him on the shoulder. "Ohh," she moaned, "I look like such an idiot!"

"What? No, you don't. Come here." He reached for her and

brought her close to his side. Another snicker escaped. "I don't suggest you go for a career in TV journalism anytime soon, though."

Jackie clicked the TV off then laid her head on his chest. After a moment, she beamed. "If I recall, you didn't exactly shine on stage either, mister." She raised her voice into a breathless falsetto, pretending to be the reporter. "Did you find your experiences as a veteran helped you rescue those children?" She batted her eyelashes. "How does it feel to be a hero?"

She lowered her voice. "Well, I dunno about that…" Tom tickled his fingers across her ribs until she burst out in giggles. She swatted his hand away. "Stop!"

"Nope, not going to happen."

She squealed as he got her in the right spot. "Stop! Tom, stop!" He flipped her over and suddenly she found herself breathless and beneath him. Staring up into his bottomless, dark brown eyes, she couldn't help imagining all the worse ways this day could have ended. "You are, y'know." At his look of confusion, she clarified, "A hero. To me and to Abby."

He leaned down, pressing his forehead against hers, and breathed deep. "I don't want to be your hero, Jackie." Shifting his weight, he reached behind him and removed a small velvet box from his back pocket. "I'd rather be your husband. Will you marry me?"

Jackie's jaw dropped. "Oh!" She pushed against him until she could scramble back up to a sitting position, then took the box and opened it. "Oh, Tom! It's beautiful! How on earth did you manage to find time to buy a ring?" She flicked the tears out of the corners of her eyes.

"I've had it for a while. Actually, I wasn't planning on giving it to you until Christmas morning, but this felt like the right time. Do you like it?" he asked, his tone painfully anxious.

"Like it? I love it!" She threw her arms around his neck and kissed him. "I love you, Tom Molsem."

"I love you, Jackie Davis." He tugged her up onto his lap. "Now, answer the damn question. Is that a yes, woman?"

"Yes!" She bounced in her excitement, and he groaned.

"Careful," he warned. He ground his hips up, letting her feel his excitement.

"Or what?" she asked mischievously.

Instead of answering, he took the ring out of the box and slid it carefully onto her finger.

"It fits," she said.

"I'll show you something else that fits." Since the box was empty, he tossed it onto the living room table and stood with her held in place. She wrapped her legs around him and nibbled his ear as he began to walk to the bedroom.

"Mmm," he groaned.

Halfway down the hallway, she said, "Wait," and slid down to stand in front of him. Together, they opened the door and peered in on Abby. It had taken longer than usual for her to go to sleep, and she'd insisted on them both staying with her until she did, but that was to be expected.

Jackie worried about what long-term effects this event was going to have on her little girl. She stood by Tom's side, thankful she'd have help for whatever came next.

"She looks peaceful," Jackie whispered. For a moment, tears threatened. "Thank goodness, she's safe."

Tom rubbed her shoulders, easing the tension he found there. "Come on. Let her rest."

Jackie stealthily stepped into the room, pulled the sheet up, then bent over and kissed Abby on the forehead. Satisfied that she was safe and secure, Jackie kept the door cracked as she left the room.

They snuck down the hallway and into the master bedroom, finally able to shut the world out behind them. He reached for her at the same time she extended her arms to him. Their lips met in the middle. He sampled her mouth, nibbling on her top lip before sucking the bottom one into his mouth.

*

"Tom..." His name sounded like a prayer coming from her. She closed her eyes as he brushed his lips over her face, kissing her forehead, her eyelids, her cheekbones, along the curve of her jawline, her chin. Her lips parted, and she pressed forward with anticipation.

Cradling her head in his hands, he kept her face tilted up to his. "Look at me." Her eyelids fluttered open, the blue of her irises the same color as the hottest part of a flame.

He took her mouth then, molding his lips to hers in a searing kiss. His tongue delved, demanded, and gave in return until she moaned. The length of her body melted against his.

His hands traveled down the length of her back until they came to the curve of her ass and he lifted her. She wrapped her legs around his waist and arched her head back as he trailed hot open-mouthed kisses down the long column of her neck.

Keeping her straddled across his lap, he sat on the mattress and ground himself against her heated core. Her breathy moans filled the room as she writhed on top of him.

He removed her nightshirt and was rewarded when her full, round breasts sprang free. His hands traced her silken skin until they cupped them. She threaded her fingers through his hair and tugged his head closer. "Tom, please," she whispered.

He was all too happy to oblige, wrapping his lips around one taut nipple and giving it a strong pull. Her head fell back, and she let out a deep groan that he could feel all the way down to his groin. He lightly bit the hard nub, letting her feel the sting of his teeth, before twirling his tongue and laving the pain away.

Turning his head, he gave her other breast equal attention, enjoying the way she rocked her weight against his hard length.

"Let me feel you," she said and reached down to pull his shirt off. It wasn't the first time she'd seen him in the light, but this time her face was lit with reverence. Her fingertips lightly traced the trail of scars that marked his body.

"I didn't fully appreciate what you must have done to earn these." She met his look. "I'm sorry you had to go through that."

He caught her hand in his and kissed her palm. "Don't be. Whatever I've done prepared me for today. I would go through it all again, and more, if it meant I could bring Abby and those other children home safely."

She held his face in her hands and kissed him deeply before pushing him back onto the mattress. Standing in front of him, she clutched the waistband of his sweatpants and dragged them off before stepping out of her own yoga pants.

Finally. No more clothes to get in the way. He peered up at her standing before him, taking his time to survey her body. "You're beautiful."

"I feel beautiful when I'm with you." She skimmed her hands over her body, pinching her nipples the way his teeth had done moments before.

He sucked in a breath, desire surging. "Come here."

*

"Come here."

Nothing could be sexier than those two words said in his passionate, gravelly voice. Hearing it made her hot.

She played coy, swiveling her hips and sliding her hands down her waist, along the flare of her hips. "Or what?"

"Woman," he warned, his voice getting deeper.

"Man." She dipped one hand between her thighs, her index finger spreading her outer lips.

He sat up and snagged her, then lifted her by the hips and pulled her down until she was once again straddling his lap. His tip flirted with her opening, dipping into her wet heat until suddenly, she wasn't teasing anymore.

"Two can play this game, you know," he said, drawing his length up along her seam.

She gasped and pressed her hips down, arching her back. "Tom."

"Uh-uh-uh..." he said, then groaned when she reached back and dug her nails into the top of his thighs.

His hands palmed her ass and spread her cheeks wide as he worked himself into her juices.

Rising up, she gripped his shoulder for balance with one hand as the other held his base steady. Her thighs burned as she guided him into her. She moaned with satisfaction when he was seated fully.

His arms were steel bands around her back, holding her tight against his chest. He was hard everywhere she was soft, and she reveled in the differences between their bodies.

When he buried his face in her neck and rocked his hips forward, each small movement sent tiny earthquakes throughout her system. Her inner muscles clenched, demanding more.

With his arms wrapped around her back, his hands holding her shoulders and keeping her in place, he surged up and into her. She cried out as he did it again and again, thrusting and filling her until every corner of her was bursting with pleasure.

Jackie strained toward him, grinding her hips down against him, meeting his every advance until they were moving in perfect harmony. A barrage of sensations flooded her until she was drowning in them.

Climax broke over them like a wave, crashing up and through her. She gasped for air, each molecule alive and thrumming. Her body clenched and stroked him until he was tumbling with her, each lost in each other's current of desire.

When Jackie was finally able to hold a coherent thought, she was draped over his chest like a shipwrecked sailor crawling to shore.

Eventually, damp sweat cooled on her skin, causing her to shiver for entirely different reasons.

Tom ran his hands down her back. "You cold?"

"A little, but I can't move."

He kissed her shoulder and sat up, carefully keeping her body pressed against his. "Let me tuck you in."

"Hmm," she mumbled, unable to say more.

He placed her on the mattress then climbed in next to her, pulling the covers up around them both. "I want to sleep for at least a week."

Curling into his heat, she sighed. "That sounds perfect," she answered before promptly slipping into oblivion.

*

"Mommy! Tom-tom! Get up! Get up!" A small knee landed in Jackie's gut, and she grunted with pain. Ugh, was that what they referred to as the solar plexus? Where was the solar plexus, anyway? Whatever it was, it certainly wasn't the most comfortable way to wake up.

"Hey, you!" she said, sitting up in the bed while strategically clutching the sheet up under her armpits. "Can you do Mommy a favor and hand me my pajamas?"

"Sure, Mommy." Abby held her yoga pants up with a quizzical look. "What are they doing over here?"

Tom snickered under the covers, and she shoved his shoulder before reaching her hand out. "Uh, Mommy got hot last night."

"I'll say," he mumbled, still hiding under the comforter.

"Listen, you," she warned under her breath.

"Sometimes, I get hot, too," Abby said. "Next time, I'll take my pajamas off, too!"

Tom choked, then sat up. "Hey, kiddo. What do you say we go make some breakfast?"

"Can we make chocolate chip pancakes?"

"You bet."

"In different shapes?"

"Whatever shape you want," he promised.

"Yay!" Abby bounced off the bed and rushed out of the room, her little feet padding down the hall.

Tom leaned over and kissed Jackie's scarlet cheek. "I take it back. This was the most perfect way to wake up."

She grinned, the bridge of her nose wrinkling. "It was, wasn't it?"

"I can't wait to see what happens on Christmas morning."

Jackie rolled her eyes. "You better get out there. You've got both of our hopes up, and I want breakfast."

"And I aim to deliver, trust me." He climbed out of bed. "Get dressed and see for yourself."

Alone in the bedroom, Jackie took a moment to reflect on all of life's secret gifts.

EPILOGUE

"IS SHE UP?" Tom whispered to Jackie.

She flung an arm over her face and tried to roll away, but he wouldn't let her. "Wha-at? Why are you talking to me this early in the morning?"

"Because it's Christmas morning, and I'm excited!"

"It's too early to be Christmas morning."

Tom sighed and let her snuggle back into her blankets. "Fine, I'll go check on Abby and see if she's up yet."

"Isn't it supposed to be the kids who wake their parents up at an insane hour?" She punched her pillow and flopped her head back down. "That's it. I'm making a new rule. No presents until a pot of coffee has been made and finished brewing!"

"Somebody's grumpy," Tom teased. He climbed from bed and slid into his slippers. "I'll get the coffee going."

He shook his head as her muffled voice floated out from under the blankets. "Thank you."

"You're welcome."

Stepping into the hallway, he was surprised to see Abby's door closed. That's funny; usually, they left it open a crack. He walked up and gently knocked on the wood.

"Hey, Sprout. What's going on in there?" He pressed the handle down, but something was blocking the door. A shiver of alarm swept through his body, and he pressed his shoulder more firmly against the door. "Abby? Open up."

"I don't wanna," came her little voice.

"You don't? Why not? Don't you know it's Christmas?" He tried the handle again.

"Nooooooo!" In any other circumstance, Tom might have acted like she was overreacting, but an undercurrent of fear laced her voice.

That's it. Tom pushed open the door and stepped into the room, noting the pile of pillows and stuffed animals on the floor. "Talk to me. What's going on?"

Abby sat up in her bed, huddled against the headboard. "Santa's mean. He took me away, and I don't want to leave you and Mommy again!"

What on earth could she be talking about? "What do you mean, Santa took you away?"

"He said that he was Santa and he was going to take me on a trip to see his kittens. He was going to let me pick one out for a Christmas gift." A sob bubbled up from Abby's throat, and it broke his heart.

He sat on the bed and gathered her up into his arms, silently cursing the bastard who had stolen her innocence. "Sweetie, I promise you, no one is ever going to take you away again. You are safe here. Mommy and I will protect you."

Tears streamed down her cheeks, and she was crying hard enough that she hiccupped. "Promise?" She shook her head. "He's not very nice. He's a bad, bad man who yells and gets red in the face. And he didn't even have any kitties!"

"Oh, my…" Jackie gasped as she stood in the doorway, her hand covering her mouth. "Hold on, one second."

She raced out of the room and returned moments later with a photo. She handed it to Tom. "He had white hair and a beard."

Tom swallowed a curse. "Your father posed as Santa when

he abducted her." Was it possible to hate the man more than he already did?

Jackie squeezed onto the mattress to sit on the other side of her daughter. "Honey, that wasn't Santa. That was a man pretending to be him, and he is never, never going to come back here. Got it?" She brushed the hair back from her daughter's temples.

Abby stuck a thumb into her mouth and snuggled onto Jackie's lap. She had fallen back into the habit since the ordeal.

After another moment, she raised her head. "If it's Christmas, does that mean there are presents?"

The spark of interest in her expression gave him fresh hope. "Uh-huh."

Jackie beamed at him over the top of her head.

He looked at the two of them. "Do you want to see them?"

Abby glowed, her eyes round with renewed excitement. "Yes!"

"Then let's go!"

The two of them raced toward the living room whooping and hollering. The Christmas tree lights sparkled, their lights dancing on the living room walls. Dozens of presents were piled under the tree. Tom and Jackie had stayed up into the wee hours of the morning wrapping last-minute gifts, each of them acknowledging the fact they were probably overcompensating.

It didn't matter. Watching Abby's face light up was enough to make him want to do it all over again. She flitted from one package to the next, clearly at a loss about where to start. "Which one do I open first?" she asked.

"I have a very special gift that I'd like to give to you, if you don't mind."

Jackie sent him a quizzical look, but he grinned and shook his head.

"Let me see!"

Tom walked over to Abby's stocking and removed a small velvet box from the top. Her face filled with curiosity. "What's in it?"

"Open it and find out."

Raising the lid, she gasped at the pretty ruby pendant that sat on a bed of white satin. "Ooh, pretty!"

"Oh, Tom…" Jackie said in a hushed tone from behind him.

"This is a very special necklace, and it means something very important."

She looked up at him. "What?"

"It means that I would like to ask you and your mommy to be a part of my family. I want to marry your mommy and consider you my daughter. Would that be okay with you?"

"You want to be my daddy?"

"One of them. You'll always have your other daddy, but I'd like to be one, too."

Abby flung her arms around his neck. "Yes!"

Tears glistened in Tom's eyes as he glanced over at Jackie. "Are you happy?" he asked.

She walked across the room and kissed him. "More than happy. I'm overjoyed. This is the greatest gift you could have given us."

"Can I wear the necklace?" Abby asked.

They both laughed, warmth and love streaming from their eyes. "Absolutely. May I help you put it on?" Tom asked.

"Yup."

Jackie spoke up. "Yes, please."

"Yes, please," she parroted back.

Very carefully, Tom placed the necklace around her neck and fixed the clasp. She straightened it out around her neck, ensuring the pendant was front and center. "Thank you," she said breathlessly. "I'm going to go look at it in the mirror!"

"Good idea," Tom agreed and watched her race from the room. She came skipping back in with a big grin. "It's beautiful! Mommy, look! Did you see?"

"I did, baby." She cuddled her daughter.

"But, if you're going to marry Mommy, what did you get her?" Abby asked.

Jackie held out her hand, letting the Christmas lights glint off the diamond ring he'd placed there.

"Ooh, that's pretty, too." Abby raised her chin. "Look, mine has red stones!"

"That's called a ruby, sweetie. It represents love and loyalty," Jackie explained.

Abby fingered the pendant and contemplated what her mom had said. Turning to Tom, she asked, "Does this mean you love me?"

Tom leaned down until he was at her level. "I absolutely love you, Abby."

She wrapped her arms around him and squeezed. "Good, because I love you, too."

His heart felt like it would burst out of his chest. After another moment, he stepped back. "Before we get to these other presents, there is something very important we have to do. It's Mommy's new rule."

"What?" Abby asked, one hand resting on her cocked hip. Tom had to bite back a grin at the amount of sass she had. It would help her bounce back from this terrible ordeal. "Mommy says we have to wait until the coffee has finished brewing before we can open presents. Want to help me make it?"

"Oh, Mom." She rolled her eyes at Jackie, and Tom let out a bark of laughter.

"Sorry, that's the rule," Jackie said, a twinkle in her eye.

"Let's do it." Abby reached out a hand and dragged the two of them into the kitchen.

An hour later, after all the gifts had been unwrapped and admired, Tom sat back enjoying the scene. With Jackie tucked comfortably under his arm, they watched Abby play with her new toys.

"Should we do it?" he asked.

She grinned. "Yes."

"Abby…" he began.

She stopped playing with the stuffed kitty in her hand and looked up. "Yes?"

"You forgot about one more present."

"I did?" She scanned the room. "I don't see another present."

"Why don't you go check in the kitchen?"

Her brow wrinkled. "Dad." She hesitated, testing the word in her mouth. "Daddy?" She shook her head. "If I get to be your daughter, I don't want to call you Tom-tom anymore. What can I call you?"

Tom swallowed past the tightness in his throat. "How about Papa?"

"Papa." She contemplated it another moment. "Papa… Papa! I like it!"

"Me too, little one." He struggled for a moment to regain his composure before speaking again. "Why don't you go check the kitchen and tell us what you find?"

Jackie sniffled and discreetly tried to wipe the tears from her cheeks.

"Good grief, woman. Are you leaking again?"

She giggled and hit his stomach with a playful punch. "Stop it. These are happy tears."

A squeal came from the other room, and Jackie sat up, sending him a smile. "Sounds like she found it."

"Oh, my gosh, you guys! How did this get here?"

"What is it?" Jackie called to her daughter, her voice laced with innocence.

"Come here and look! Oh, my gosh! Oh, my gosh! Papa, Mommy, come look at my new bike!"

"You got a new bike?" Tom asked as they walked into the kitchen. Jackie covered her mouth with a hand.

"I did! And look, it's red. Exactly like I asked him."

Jackie placed a hand on Abby's head as Tom crouched down to

inspect the cherry-red bicycle sitting in the middle of the kitchen. "Asked who?"

"Santa! I asked Santa for a bike and he gave it to me!" She skipped and hopped with excitement. "And look! It even has the little white basket I asked for... and streamers!"

"This looks like a magnificent bike," Tom agreed. "I can't wait to see you ride it."

"Hey, there's even a new helmet right here on the dining room table. And it matches! Ohh, I love the red flowers on it."

"You're going to be the most stylish rider in the neighborhood," Jackie assured her.

"In the state," Tom said.

"In the whole world!" Abby finished. She froze, her face a mask of confusion.

Tom and Jackie exchanged a concerned look. "What's wrong, sweetie?" she asked.

"How did he get it in here? It wasn't here when we were in the kitchen making coffee. I would have seen it."

"That is the magic of Christmas," Tom informed her.

OTHER BOOKS BY SATIN RUSSELL

<u>The Harper Sister Series</u>

Secret Hunger
Secret Need
Secret Dream – Coming soon?

ABOUT THE AUTHOR

Satin was an avid reader who wanted to either be an English teacher, librarian, or author growing up. So, of course she became a financial advisor. On the eve of her 36th birthday, she realized life was short, and decided to follow her dream. Now, she's published the first two books in her romantic suspense trilogy called The Harper Sisters, as well as this holiday novella set in the same universe.

Satin lives in Massachusetts and is married to the love of her life, a man who literally flew halfway around the world for her. When she isn't writing, she loves reading, supporting fellow authors (especially self-published ones,) traveling, and photography. You can follow her adventures at satinrussell.com, on Twitter @SatinRussell, or Instagram @SatinR.

Satin loves to hear from her readers! You can email her at satinrussell@hotmail.com.

If you liked this book, please consider leaving a review and supporting Satin as a new author.

Thank you!

Made in the
USA
Middletown, DE